Balgay H

10 dark tales

George Burton

ISBN 978-0-9927889-5-7
Published by Kelsoprint
Printed by Bell & Bain, Glasgow

Acknowledgements

My sincere thanks to the following for reviewing the stories, making helpful suggestions, and giving me the confidence to publish:

The Nethergate Writers

Mary Burton

Mike Landay

Special thanks to my brother Joe Burton, who proofread and edited this book. Thanks to Dave Houghton for the cover and inside photos and to Alison Houghton for her help with publicity. Thanks to the Local History Centre at Dundee Central Library for permission to use the image at the beginning of "South Lodge"

TABLE OF CONTENTS

www.socratesthesnail.co.uk

Contact the author on his blog

www.georgeandmaryadventure.wordpress.com

1
BANDSTAND

Bert was a drunk. He hadn't always been a drunk, no, not at all, but now he had fallen into that category of retired people who go to the pub fairly regularly, maybe two three times a week, and drink pretty much every night at home. That hadn't been possible when he'd worked at D. C. Thomson's ten years earlier, swopping early shift with back shift and nights, typesetting the Courier, the Evening Telegraph or The Sporting Post. OK, he used to take a few on a Friday night, either in the Duke of Edinburgh with his pal Ian or in between numbers when he played trumpet with The Dudhope Five in the Jazz Club at the top of Parker Street. He was careful of course not to go beyond four or five pints, after which he could easily start to miss his notes, something that didn't go down well with the crowd who expected him to be Dundee's Satchmo. Those were good days, with steady wages, extra pocket money with the band and not a care in the world.

But marriage had put an end to most of that as he was bullied by his wife into earning more, staying in, no more trumpet practice, a reduction in his drinking and the constant nagging to keep her in a way only she had been used to. That's why Bert had held on so desperately to his Friday nights at the Jazz Club despite his wife's objections. Four hours free to express himself with the band and down a few pints in company he knew and liked helped balance the oppressive atmosphere that had quickly engulfed his life after their shotgun wedding. The resentment Bert felt when he learned it had been a false alarm stayed with him all his days and he never stopped believing his wife had set him up.

Yet it had all totally changed within twelve years. His wife's sudden demise from an attack of pleurisy was a blessed relief for him, but he was rocked back on his heels by the passing of both his parents within weeks of each other during the Hong Kong 'flu epidemic of 1968. And suddenly Bert was alone. He moved into his parents' house on Blackness Road, paid off the small mortgage with some of the insurance money, likewise bought a brand-new Ford Cortina Mk II and went back to his former carefree existence. Now quite comfortably well-off, he decided to retire from D. C. Thomson's and just enjoy life, including taking up his trumpet again, at least at home.

Enjoying life however also translated into spending a lot of time with old friends, and new friends who had heard of his recent financial good fortune, in the Charleston Bar on the other side of Balgay and Lochee Parks. Admittedly the walk through the parks to and fro several times a week allowed him to keep his legs in good order, not that he'd ever been what might be described as unfit, but he didn't seem to be aware of the amount of lager and whisky chasers he was now consuming at the pub.

Bert's route home was always the same, rain or shine. Once he'd been shown the door at the "Charlie Bar" just after 10 p.m. he would walk along Charleston Drive as far as Lochee Park then head south through the park and under the spooky bridge, past the bandstand and down the side of Victoria Hospital to Kelso Street, whose famous steps brought him within 100 yards of his house on

Blackness Road. It was a trek of about half-an-hour. The darkness and isolation of the road through the park at such a late hour had never bothered Bert, but, even with a gallon of lager inside him, he kept his eyes peeled and would proceed with caution if he heard anything unusual.

One Friday night, shortly before his sixty-second birthday, Bert reached the high point of the path directly under the bridge on his way home. He stopped and listened. There wasn't a soul in sight but he could just make out some noise ahead of him down by the bandstand. Kids having a carry-on? He listened again. No, this noise was rhythmic, as if musical, but it kept coming and going, so Bert couldn't fix on it. He continued down the hill, noting that the noise got slightly louder but then faded altogether when he reached the steps to the hospital path. He made his way back to the house without incident, poured himself a nightcap (two fingers of The Macallan 10-year-old), munched his way through two bags of crisps, and slowly fell asleep in his armchair with some of his favourite tunes wandering around inside his head.

With a change in the Licensing Laws in Scotland recently enacted, Sunday was a new opportunity for Bert to take up his place at a table near the bar and play a few games of dominoes with his pals. Thankfully, having to concentrate just a bit on playing the "bones" in his hand, he drank only about half of his normal quota of lager so he was a good deal more sober than most Friday or Saturday nights. Taking his usual route home, he became aware for a second time of some kind of rhythmic beating sound as he approached the bandstand and indeed paused briefly to check if perhaps speakers had recently been installed high up on the metal pillars. Bert failed to find anything new on the structure so continued on his way and was soon back in his armchair with his Macallan. All was well.

That Monday morning after his bacon and eggs, Bert happened to be looking for a document, his

M.O.T. for the Cortina, in the chest of drawers in one of the spare bedrooms when his eye was drawn to a glimpse of sunlight reflecting off something next to the big armchair. When he went over to investigate, he discovered his old trumpet in its open case. That was strange. Why would he have put the instrument back without closing the case? And when had he last had the trumpet out? He'd long since given up on daily or even weekly practice and he struggled to remember the last time he'd played it in the house. God, it was so annoying not being able to remember the most basic of things, like where he'd put his Courier or when his appointment was with the dentist. But he could still play the trumpet as he proved when he took the old instrument from its case, held it lovingly to his lips and blew out the opening bars to "Love Walked In" by Miles Davis. He missed a few notes and gave up at the solo but it brought a smile to his face. He could still get a tune out of the old thing. But that was enough for the moment so he put the instrument back in the green velvet folds of its case and closed it firmly.

When he returned to his living-room, Bert went over to his dad's old record player, chose an album from the rack below and placed the needle delicately on the vinyl. As always, when he wasn't quite in the mood for some jazz, Bert put on a Beatles' album, this time the iconic "Sgt. Pepper's Lonely Hearts Club Band". As the title track started to play, Bert couldn't resist scanning the famous album cover, trying to identify as many of the characters as he could. Yes, he could still spot Tony Curtis, Edgar Allan Poe, Marlon Brando and Lewis Carroll, and of course he was pleased to note that Ringo Starr had a gleaming trumpet held in his right hand. He smiled, but quickly changed his expression to one of surprise when his eyes fell on the stone bust to the right of the bass drum.

Now he'd read years earlier in the New Musical Express that this was a bust of a person unknown and had been brought by John Lennon from his house in Weybridge to be used in the cover photo of the album. But the more Bert stared at the bust, the more he began to see definite traces of someone he knew very well. He checked in the large mirror above the living-room fireplace. Hmmm. The eyes and nose were quite similar to his, although the mouth wasn't right and the hairstyle couldn't match Bert's balding pate. He thought it strange however that he'd never noticed this similarity before and when he put the cover back down, he remained unsettled.

By this time the album had reached the last track on side one, but Bert hurried over to the record player and lifted the needle just as the opening bars of "Being for The Benefit of Mr. Kite" filled the air. No, that was one song he didn't want to hear, as he had always considered it an aberration among the almost perfect anthology of songs by The Beatles. He had never understood why Lennon and McCartney had included this circus tune on their finest album and he preferred to simply bypass the song and turn the record over. That was better. Time for a dram.

That Friday was to be Bert's birthday celebration in the Charleston Lounge, the far side of which he'd hired out for his friends and their wives. He was expecting about thirty people to show up and had paid the landlord to lay on sausage rolls, sandwiches, Scotch eggs and even some of that fancy Quiche everyone was talking about. The first round would be on him, but after that he didn't expect to have to put his hand in his pocket. He checked all was organised when he was in on Wednesday evening and his party was the talk of the pub. He ended up inviting one or two extra people who happened to be in the bar that evening, including a guy called Joe and his rather angry-looking son Kevin, whom his father described as having just left school and wondering about maybe getting a job somewhere. Kevin appeared less than interested.

Bert's walk home was just as it always was, except for the strange noises he heard again as he approached the bandstand. He thought he could make out a French Horn and maybe even a weird kind of a Trombone beat, but it was very confused and the slight chill of the evening pushed him to get home as quickly as possible and warm his insides with a nice whisky. Back home on Blackness Road, Bert picked up the album cover he'd left out the previous time and had another good look at the characters on the front, but almost immediately his eyes picked out the stone bust. Maybe that mouth wasn't as different from his as he'd previously thought, and those eyes and nose were definitely similar. He couldn't quite believe he hadn't noticed that on an album he'd had for 10 years and more. This time the record was returned to its inner cover and slid back into the album. Bert said goodnight to all the characters and replaced the album in its rack.

Friday began with the postman delivering a dozen or so birthday cards which Bert read almost immediately. All were from friends who couldn't make the party that evening, but he'd known that in advance and was untroubled by the excuses. Nice of them to remember! After breakfast, he took the 73 bus into town, had a wander around the McManus Galleries and a coffee in the Wellgate Centre while waiting for the highly popular nursery rhyme clock to strike twelve. After the display, he did some shopping in the newly-opened Market Hall and was back home for lunch by one-thirty. A nap followed then it was time to get ready for his party. Boy, he was going to enjoy this!

Dressed in his best trousers and shirt and wearing his D. C. Thomson tie for the first time since his sixtieth, Bert broke the habit of a lifetime and took a taxi over to the Charlie Bar, ensuring he would be in the lounge before any of his guests. That also gave him time to get a couple of single malts down him to calm his unexpected nerves. But once his guests started to arrive bang on 7 p.m. he was able to relax and the evening progressed much as he'd hoped it would. Almost everyone invited turned up, the food was really good and the drink was in plentiful supply. Only one small incident soured the celebrations and that was when he accidently spilled a pint of heavy over Kevin, Joe's boy. Unfortunately, Kevin reacted badly to his best clothes being soaked, grabbed Bert by the collar and called him a clumsy old prick. As Bert tried to apologise, Joe came over and smacked his son hard on the back of the head, daring him to ever say that again to one of his friends and then sending him home to get changed. Red-faced and seething with anger, Kevin stared menacingly at both his father and Bert, muttered something they couldn't quite catch then turned and stormed out of the lounge.

The incident was quickly forgotten however as one of the lady guests, no doubt lubricated on one too many vodkas and cokes, grabbed a microphone from behind the bar and burst into song, encouraging the other patrons to join in. Soon the Charleston Lounge was echoing to "The Road and the Miles to Dundee," "I belong to Glasgow" and "The Northern Lights of old Aberdeen", none of them anything like the records. Even Bert took his turn with the mic and belted out a passable version of Louis Armstrong's "What a Wonderful World." It turned out to be quite the show-stopper and reminded Bert of some of the better nights at the Parker Street Jazz Club. He had forgotten how much he loved the applause.

When closing time came, everyone left having had a good evening, and several of the guests offered Bert a lift, but he insisted he would stay to the last then call a taxi as he had a lot of presents (mainly bottles) to carry home. The plan however came unstuck when the barman who was phoning for a taxi told Bert he'd have to wait three-quarters of an hour for one, as the town was very busy after a big concert at the Caird Hall. Despite being slightly the worse for wear, Bert insisted on leaving his presents behind the bar until the next day and doing what he did most normal nights to get home. He would walk through the park.

It wasn't quite walking however and more of a stagger, but he managed to keep on his feet despite a couple of near disasters and made it into the park where he stumbled up the slight incline to the bridge. The downslope to the bandstand proved equally if not more difficult to negotiate but Bert made it down to the redwood tree which he often liked to punch to remind himself of his youth. After two very enjoyable swings at the soft bark, he decided it was time for a pee. Fumbling at the zip of his trousers, Bert eventually got himself in order and gave a deep sigh of relief as he started to empty his aching bladder. So he never saw his assailant approach nor swing the branch towards his head. Indeed he hardly felt the blow at all.

Everything went black and he fell to the ground, cracking his forehead wide open on a rock.

When he next opened his eyes, a familiar figure was bent over him offering a hand to help him get up. Bert was puzzled for a second then realised it was someone dressed in George Harrison's red uniform from the cover of Sgt. Pepper's.

-Hello Bert. I'm Brian and I'm the Bandmaster. Now that you've passed, I am allowed to offer you the position of third trumpet player in the band. It's a splendid opportunity, given that our first trumpet player has only just moved up. That leaves a vacancy and we've been waiting for you. Would you care to join us?

-Now that I've passed? Bert said. Join your band? Is this a joke?

- Sorry to surprise you with all of this, Bert, but that lad Kevin just killed you as we knew he would. Unfortunately, as your record on good works isn't perfect, you can't go directly up there, if you catch my drift. Have you heard of Purgatory? No? Well, it's the state you stay in until you've served your time making up for all your peccadilloes. There's no saying how long it'll last but promotion comes around eventually and you get to go up. We all do. In the meantime, you can join the band here if you want and play the trumpet for a few nights, or months, or years. We play every night from twelve until six in the morning, here on the Balgay bandstand. Only we, the band members, can hear what we play and it's a bit repetitive but it's better than just standing in a queue.

Bert glanced down to see his bloodied and inert body lying on the grass next to the punch tree.

-Do I have any other options? he asked.

- Not really, came the reply from the Bandmaster. I think you should join. You get a nice uniform and I know how much you like playing music.

-OK, count me in. Is it all brass band stuff?

-Oh, not at all. You're going to be playing The Beatles.

-Great! Which songs do we play?

21

-It doesn't work like that, Bert. You only play one song and one song only. And you play it continuously until your time is up. It's the same for everyone. In my case, I have to conduct "The Day we went to Bangor" for the whole 6 hours every night. Sometimes it's genuine torture.

-So, do I get to choose what I'll be playing? Bert enquired.

- Oh no, my friend. You must remember that this is Purgatory, so it's not meant to be all that pleasant. The suffering is repetitive: that's the whole point.

-In that case, do you have any idea what I'll be playing for such a long, long time?

-Yes I do, Bert. It's The Beatles' "Being for the Benefit of Mr. Kite"!

2
GRAVEYARD

When Jillian ran into the cemetery that night, the tears were still streaming down her face, mixing with the rain that had been drenching her for the previous ten minutes since she'd left Tommy's house. Not that she noticed it much. The chaos in her head was at full pitch still and she literally had no idea where she was going or what she needed to do next. Stopping the pain was all that mattered: turning the clock back to that moment just before Tommy told her they were finished. She wanted that to have not happened. To have continued to be his girlfriend for ever, to walk along the road hand in hand each and every day with the boy she surely loved: to feel his arms around her, protecting her from the world she so distrusted, from the mum who didn't understand her and from the others at school who called her a freak.

And now suddenly, Tommy had decided it was time for them to split, after only three weeks and four days, the most amazing twenty-five days of her fifteen years on the planet. Being with Tommy was better than her summer holiday in Portsoy with auntie Dorothy, better than her birthday party three years ago in the Jimmy Shand pub just up the road, better than her first ever kiss from Tony Brown on the coach trip to Codona's in first year. No, nothing compared to the complete happiness of Tommy McDonald asking her to be his girl and then being with him every single day since. They didn't call her a freak so much when she was with Tommy and she'd even been invited to a party with him last week, the very first time she'd met up with all those smug girls outside of school, all eye-brows and fake tan and dressed like sluts. They were all dreadful and Tommy had said how he hated them all looking exactly the same and preferred her because she was a Goth.

She wanted to know why he'd changed his mind so quickly. But her brain simply wasn't ready for logic or straight-thinking just now. It was screaming "No! No! No!" So much so that she gave voice to one of them and let forth a blood-curdling roar of pain and sorrow which spread out across the empty graveyard, bouncing off the gravestones all the way up Balgay Hill. It wasn't enough and it didn't help. She screamed once more, eyes shut tight and head shaking violently from side to side, but the silence of the graveyard at midnight absorbed her agonised lament and sucked it down into the wet ground. There was no-one there to help, no-one to dry her tears or tell her it would be ok and Tommy would take her back. She had been rejected once again, just like she'd been almost all her life

And that last thought, the realisation that nobody cared, that she really was alone in the world brought from deep within her another emotion to counter the hurt. Anger. It stopped the tears and told her it was time to stop letting herself be treated like that, to be abused, rejected, teased, hurt, and left alone to lick her wounds. Jillian closed her eyes and tilted her head backwards, daring the rain to do its worst. She hated them all, Tommy, her mum, the girls at school and those who lived near her in Menzieshill, even her teachers. But most of all Tommy. Tommy McDonald. He would have to pay for the hurt she was now having to endure. He couldn't get off with what he'd done by dumping her. No, that wasn't fair. She'd make sure she trashed his name in any way she could, even if it meant making stuff up like forcing her to steal money from her mum's purse to buy fags, or hitting her because she wouldn't do what he wanted. Yeah, she'd get even.

The anger was doing its job and masking the pain of no longer having Tommy McDonald as her boyfriend. And then she saw it, glinting briefly in the reflection of one of the street lights on Glamis Road. The name McDonald. On a wee white gravestone. It was just the name, but the rage had consumed her and she automatically transferred some engraved letters into the boy she'd just lost. She ran over to the stone, bent down and spat on it.

-There, Tommy McDonald! Take that! I fucking hate you, you bastard! I hope you die slowly and painfully and end up in here where I can come over every day and dance on your ugly face. You're not going to get away with treating me like shit. Just you wait!

But she wasn't satisfied. If anything, the fact that her screaming rage was left unanswered in the silence of the graveyard only served to worsen her feelings of hatred towards everybody and everything around her and left her searching for an outlet for her fury. And that little white gravestone became an instant victim. Jillian lifted her foot and kicked with her heel at the name "McDonald" etched in a semi-circle around the top of the stone. The memorial didn't flinch. She aimed a second harder kick at the name. Still it didn't move. But the third furious kick caused the stone to rock back slightly. Jillian screamed again, half in fury and half in triumph at having made it move, even if only a little bit. Now the weakness was revealed, she leapt forward and grabbed the top of the stone with her two sodden hands and shook with all her might, while continuing to curse and swear and pledge to bring ill down onto the whole McDonald clan.

As the stone was only about two feet high, she managed to get it to rock back and forth on its concrete plinth until it reached tipping point, finally falling backwards with a quiet thud and embedding itself into the wet ground. Jillian's rage abated just long enough for her to read the inscription now staring up at her:

"In memory of our little darling, REBECCA, born 17/02/18, died 10/03/21, taken from us too soon, now with daddy forever in heaven."

A tiny instant of regret may have passed through Jillian's heart, but her eyes quickly fixed back on the engraving of the name McDonald, inciting her to jump up and down with both feet on the toppled stone, all the while continuing to utter the most awful profanities. Maybe it was just as well Tommy wasn't there. As the rain poured down in biblical fashion, Jillian finally brought her rant to an end with a last indignant stamp and stood on the flat white stone, catching her breath. The hundreds of other gravestones stood there silently, as if shocked by the ferocity of the girl's temper. They had seen thousands of mourners weeping and even crying out in grief but they had never witnessed the fury of a young teenager scorned by the boy she had loved. Her pain seemed unbearable.

-Young lady, what are you doing?

Jillian spun round, surprised to hear another voice in what she thought was an empty cemetery. Standing by the next gravestone, a much taller, shiny, black stone, was a man dressed in a white suit and barefoot.

-Where did you come from? asked the girl.

-I saw what you did, young lady. What is your name?

-Jillian, so what's it to you? Are you one of those pervs they've been telling us about at school? Creeping around and watching us? Well, don't even bother, Mister. I'm seriously pissed off and definitely not in the mood for a graveyard chat, so off you pop and leave me alone.

-Of course I will, the man replied. Immediately after you apologise and put the headstone back where it's meant to be. What you've just done here is very bad, you know. Some might say unforgivable. That little girl will be so upset at having her memorial toppled. Do you even know who she is? Who she was? We can't let teenagers like you run around wild damaging our headstones just for fun.

-We? Who's we? Jillian asked, confused and annoyed at how the conversation was going.

-Us, the man said, indicating with his right hand that Jillian turn round and look. And when she did, she could hardly believe her eyes. For behind her, interspersed between the dozens of graves in the immediate area, was a whole crowd of people. All dressed in white and barefoot. All staring at her in a very disapproving way. None of them were moving and none made to speak, but they all looked on at her, waiting.

-We're like the Friends of Balgay Cemetery, as it were, the man continued. We watch over it at night. Rain or no rain, no matter what the weather. This is a holy place and we keep it that way. There's not much we can do if some of the headstones fall over in the wind or crumble with old age, but we try to make sure the newer ones do their job and stay in place. That's why we need you to stand Rebecca's headstone back upright on its plinth. So come on, get to work. You knocked it down so you can put it back where it was.

Jillian's rage had naturally been calmed considerably by her sudden encounter with the Friends of Balgay and deep down she began to regret her act of vandalism. But she was determined not to be intimidated by the group. Nor by anyone as it happened. No, not any more. Tommy was the last straw. She'd be doing things on her own terms from now on. Nonetheless, she made a cursory attempt at lifting the white stone, found it nigh on impossible to budge, and quickly gave up.

-Sorry, Mister. Can't oblige. The stone's too fucking heavy and slippy. No chance I can lift it on my own. You'll have to help me.

-I can't, he replied. None of us can help with the lifting. You have to do it yourself. Try again.

Jillian considered whether she should just walk away at that point and leave the Friends to put the headstone back, but her conscience was just awake enough to tell her to have another go. This time she managed to raise the top of the memorial a couple of inches off the ground before her feet slipped on the muddy grass and the heavy stone thumped back down, trapping her fingers in the soft ground. She winced in pain and let out a stream of expletives, kneeling in the mud.

-Fuck this, she said, scrambling back to her feet. That's it, I'm done here.

But as Jillian turned to leave, she saw that the group had all silently come much nearer and that she was now completely encircled by them. She thought about pushing her way through them but something about their quiet demeanour told her they were unlikely to let her do that. She turned to the man.

-So, what am I supposed to do now? I can't move it back up and none of you will help. Oh my God! This is mental! Look, I'll tell you what, I'll come back tomorrow evening with a friend to help. My pal Kirsty is as strong as an ox. She'll be able to lift it, I'm sure. Ok? Now I need to get home out of this pissing rain.

-I don't think you quite understand, young lady. You have no choice in the matter. Only you can repair the damage you've caused and you can't leave here until you've done it. You'll just have to try harder.

-I've already told you I'm done here tonight, the girl shouted, her previous rage reigniting. Now get out of my fucking way you perv.

The teenager stretched out her arms to push past the man but, to her shock and horror, they went right through him instead. Her balance lost, Jillian crashed to the ground, rolling over in the mud. As the man stepped aside, she saw through the downpour that there was a little girl in a white dress standing next to the overturned headstone, looking up at the man.

-Yes, daddy, she deserves it. She hurt my stone and she won't put it back. Do it! Do it!

The following day, the Dundee Evening Telegraph splashed the headline of a local teenage schoolgirl killed in an accident the previous night in Balgay Cemetery, crushed by a large black headstone.

3
SOUTH LODGE

The young woman stared at the envelope, re-reading her own name and address:

Miss Emelia J. Hetherington

45 Sutton Mews

Twickenham

London

Was this the first letter she had ever received? She felt almost sure that indeed it was. For the first time in weeks, a genuine feeling of excitement pushed away the melancholy that she had feared would never lift. She could wait no longer, so gently lifted the ornate letter-knife her late mother had brought her back from Versailles, and ever so carefully slit open the missive. Her nostrils were immediately assailed by the strong scent of lavender from within and as she delicately pulled the letter from its envelope, several small, mauve petals fell onto the writing-desk at which she was seated. She unfolded the single sheet of paper and began to read:

"My dearest Emelia,

How can I even begin to express the terrible sadness I feel at the recent events which must have brought you such unspeakable grief and pain. To have to deal with the loss of your dear father, cut down in the service of his country so far from home in South Africa, would be enough to push most daughters to the edge of reason, but to lose your mother, our beloved Eve, within the space of 3 months to that accursed tuberculosis, is indeed a blow from which you will do well to recover.

And it is to that end that I write to you now. But first of all, I must apologise deeply for not attending your mother's funeral in Twickenham nor the memorial service for your father in Whitehall. I am afraid that an indisposition of my own has kept me confined to the house here in Dundee and were it not for the care afforded to me by my housekeeper Precious, I fear I might well have succumbed to whatever has been ailing me this while. Deo gratias! They tell me it is a disorder of the blood, but that rest, good food and stimulating company will restore my spirits and allow me to return to my daily routine.

I have nonetheless realised of late that we as cousins may be of direct benefit to one another by spending some time together up here in Scotland. It would afford you the opportunity to escape from the lonely confines of your family residence now that you are the sole occupant, and it will give us the chance to celebrate together both your imminent twenty-first birthday when you come of age and the turn of the century in six weeks' time. I am delighted to tell you that, due to the sudden demise of its previous owner, I have been able to purchase the South Lodge of Balgay Park, a beautiful gatehouse with stunning views over the park and down to the river Tay which, as you will know, reaches the North Sea at Dundee. There is plenty of space for us in the lodge and you can use the bedroom at the top of the tower if you so wish, a room overlooking the park and open to sunlight for almost the entire day.

Dearest Emelia, please tell me you will travel up next month in time for your birthday. It will be such a delight and will lift whatever clouds have been hiding the sun from our lives of late.

I await your reply impatiently

Your loving cousin, Henrietta."

Emelia made her mind up almost at once. The thought of spending the winter alone in London and dealing with her late parents' extensive affairs day after day was enough to drive her to distraction, and here was Cousin Henrietta giving her the perfect opportunity to avoid what she had been dreading. And why not? What held her there in the capital now that her parents were gone?

Emelia therefore wrote back to her older cousin accepting her kind invitation and then made the necessary arrangements to travel by train from London to Edinburgh and thereafter on to Dundee. She would do so on the second Sunday in December, the tenth, meaning she would be settled in Dundee with her cousin a full two weeks before Christmas and three before her important birthday which coincided with the beginning of the twentieth century, a huge cause for widespread celebration. She also asked Henrietta to meet her at Dundee Station so that they might take a carriage up to Balgay together, especially were it to snow, which was always likely so far north.

The melancholy which had afflicted the young woman since the loss of her beloved parents did not of course instantly evaporate but it did gradually appear to lift somewhat, helped in no small measure by the excitement of her upcoming trip to Scotland. The intervening weeks passed relatively quickly with no additional burdens falling upon her young shoulders and, the day of her journey, she awoke to blue skies and an unusually mild climate. This heralded a pleasant few hours of reading while one of the great locomotives sped her the four hundred or so miles north to Edinburgh Waverley Station. A smaller, more sedate train took her the rest of the way to Dundee and she thrilled to the point of not daring to breathe as it crossed the Tay Bridge which had collapsed almost exactly twenty years earlier.

Safely arrived at Dundee Station, there followed an emotional reunion of the two cousins before they mounted a Hansom carriage which climbed the slope to the west of the city and deposited both women outside the South Lodge at the end of Balgay Road. Emelia instantly fell in love with the spectacular gatehouse and admired its design from several different angles before Henrietta ushered her inside, leaving Precious and the carriage driver to bring in her guest's luggage, two small chests and a travel bag. The two cousins were immediately served a cup of tea and some fresh scones with butter and a local jam before Emelia was taken up the spiral staircase to her room at the top of the imposing tower. The room was small in comparison to her bedroom back in London, but its rounded walls and wonderful views south more than compensated for its lack of space. Over a low-key dinner that evening, the cousins caught up on their separate lives in such different parts of the country, and Emelia retired to her room as happy as she could possibly have hoped to be. Her sleep was both long and dreamless.

In the approach to the final Christmas of the century, the cousins spent all their waking hours together, rekindling the family bond they had once had during their upbringing in the capital. However, Henrietta's short-lived marriage at the age of eighteen had taken her away from London and deposited her in the Scottish town famous for its jute, jam and journalism. On their constitutionals, the cousins avoided the smog of Dundee itself, preferring to visit the fruit-laden countryside of Strathmore by carriage or a short trip in the train to the county town of Perth. But much of their time was spent simply walking around the parks and hills of Balgay which provided such an excellent escape from the bustle of the busy town and the noise of the jute mills.

And Mother Nature even deigned to give them their secret wish of a heavy snowfall on Christmas Eve, affording them the opportunity to pick their way through the blanket of white as they made their way down to St. Andrew's Cathedral for Midnight Mass. On their return by Hansom cab, Precious served them hot chestnuts with a glass of port to warm their insides as they sat by the big fire in the living-room and opened their presents to each other. When they retired that night, both felt that life had taken a turn for the better and that happier days were ahead.

Precious again worked her culinary magic on Christmas Day, serving up a yuletide feast fit for royalty and it was no surprise that both cousins decided to take the air in the park to aid their digestion. The snow was still lying thick on the paths, slowing the pace of their walk up towards the beautiful pavilion and the magnificent Balgay Bridge, built only twenty-seven years earlier, which spanned the natural gorge between the hill and the new cemetery.

As they reached the unoccupied North Lodge beyond the bridge, they were suddenly aware of rapidly-falling darkness accompanied by a noticeable drop in temperature, so hastened to retrace their steps back to the South Lodge and the cosy fire awaiting them. While Henrietta chattered on about how lovely life was now in Scotland, Emelia found herself battling a distinct unease that had descended upon her as they made their way through the gorge, and the disquiet continued to set her on edge as they turned left and made for home. Small, almost insignificant noises – a dog barking, a twig snapping, snow falling off a branch – caused her to start and pull her cousin in closer than they already were, arm in arm. Henrietta scolded her for being so sensitive, but Emelia was not entirely telling her cousin the truth when she said she was sorry for being so silly.

Safely back at the South Lodge and it being Christmas night, the cousins indulged themselves with not one but two glasses of port and Henrietta joked that if they kept that up, they would soon be joining the ranks of Dundee's infamous drunk women, well-known for dominating their households and letting their hair down at the weekends after so many long hours in the jute mills. Unsurprisingly, Emelia found herself feeling the effects of a second glass, excused herself and retired for the night to the tower bedroom with one of Sir Walter Scott's novels. After only a dozen pages or so, her eyes began to droop, and soon she was fast asleep with the book still open in her hands.

That night, her sleep was anything but dreamless, with a chaos of random thoughts and images invading the blackness of her mind. Noises pierced her slumber – another dog, this time growling not barking, a door slamming shut, footsteps on the floor below, a cry of pain then a whimper – causing her at least twice to open her eyes and listen. Both times however there was nothing but the sound of the bitter north wind rattling the casement of the tower window, leaving Emelia to return to her sleep after only a few troubled moments.

The following day, at breakfast, Emelia was slow to join conversation with her cousin, who appeared more animated than ever, probably after such a good night's sleep brought on by those two glasses of port. Her cheeks were ruddier than Emelia had ever seen them and she commented that the sharpness of the winter in Scotland was clearly doing Henrietta good. Her cousin laughed and pointed to her unusually dishevelled coiffure which she claimed she had not been able to restore yet, having risen late and fearing she might anger Precious by being tardy for breakfast. Both women found the topic highly amusing and they ended up giggling like schoolgirls.

After breakfast, Henrietta took Emelia into the small sitting-room and apprised her of her plans for the latter's birthday celebration which would be on the last day of the year, as well as that of the nineteenth century. But as they sat talking of the arrangements, there was a loud knock at the front door and Precious came in to say that there was a policeman who wished to ask them a question or two if that was convenient. Intrigued, Henrietta had him brought to the sitting-room, the constable thanked them for their time and accepted the invitation to take a seat. He refused the offer of a cup of tea and in a polite manner begged to be allowed to explain.

The constable had to call on all of his prowess with the English language to avoid distressing the two women as he recounted how a man and his pet terrier had been found torn to pieces under the Balgay Bridge late on Christmas night. The attack had been of astonishing brutality, he explained, although he left out all of the gory details lest it might cause the women to swoon. Prints in the snow nearby led the police to believe that a large dog had been the assailant and further prints showed that the beast had run to and from the bridge right the way down to the South Lodge. As there were no witnesses and no-one else appeared to have heard anything, the policeman asked the women if they had heard anything unusual the night before. Henrietta gave a firm no and, although she hesitated a moment in her reply, Emelia followed suit, fearing that recounting what she had thought to have heard might bring ridicule upon her. The constable thanked the women for their help and, with a final warning to avoid walking in the park after dark, Precious ushered him to the door and out onto the main drive through the park.

The cousins spent some time discussing the horrific incident but, as there was no local paper that day to give them details, they were left to speculate as to which kind of dog could possibly have perpetrated such an outrage. They agreed that a very large hound must have been the attacker and resolved to stay at home each day after three in the afternoon when darkness would start to descend, as it did every mid-winter in Scotland. The next few days consisted of walks in the surrounding area, afternoon tea in the beautiful Queen's Hotel and an excellent trip by train to the little fishing port of Arbroath, where they were able to observe the fleet unloading their catches of haddock and cod. Nonetheless, on the advice of the constable, the cousins made a point of being at home before sunset and resisted any urge to go walking after dinner, even though a thaw had set in and the snowfall of Christmas Eve had completely disappeared.

The last day of the century saw the two cousins celebrate Emelia's coming of age with a lavish luncheon, again at the Queen's Hotel, while the town put on a show of optimism for the future with marching bands and street performers. Henrietta gave her younger cousin a musical trinket box as a birthday present and Precious baked her a lemon sponge cake, a slice of which was so exquisite that both women simply had to have a second one with their supper. When Emelia retired to her room, she sat momentarily by the tower window and looked out over the river Tay which reflected the full moon on its calm surface, painting a picture which brought tears to her eyes. She could not have envisaged such happiness prior to leaving London and her deceased parents behind. Emelia changed into her nightgown and slipped into the cosy bed which Precious had warmed with a bed-warmer filled with hot coals. Unbeknownst to her, downstairs, Henrietta and Precious were sipping on a glass of cherry brandy over a few hands of gin rummy. Sleep did not appear to be part of their immediate intentions, and they were still playing cards when a multitude of church bells from all over Dundee heralded in the twentieth century. They toasted the New Year together and settled down for a night away from their beds.

When Emelia awoke, late that morning, she was astounded to find herself naked and lying on the Persian rug next to the tower window. As she hurried to cover up her modesty, her mind spinning in utter confusion, she caught herself in the dressing-table mirror and gasped in horror. Her face was covered with blood! She was searching frantically for the source of the wound when there was a knock at the bedroom door and Henrietta and Precious came in, smiling.

-Emelia dear, do not fret, said Henrietta calmly. Precious will tend to you at once and you can then return to bed. You will be totally exhausted after your first kill.

4
DAILY WALK

- That's me off on my walk, love.

- OK, pet, take care. Have you got your phone?

- Yeah, phone, wallet and keys, and headphones in my backpack.

- Good. Have fun.

- Don't think it'll rain. It's meant to stay fair. See you in an hour or so.

-Have you taken your tablets? Don't want you dying on me.

- Yeah, all done, thank you.

- Oh, by the way, if you pass a shop, nip in and get some kitchen roll, please. I forgot to buy it when I was in Lidl this morning.

- OK, but I'm not promising I'll remember. Bye, love!

"Right... should I nip back for my woolly hat? Nah! It's not meant to be so cold today. Here we are, the slowest lift in Scotland. It was good having Cordelia here for the weekend. Amazing how her speech has come on. 'Grandad Jim too 'piky'. She really doesn't like me kissing her when I haven't had a shave. But we're always so knackered once she's away back home. Still the best baby ever, though. Never known a child that sleeps 11 hours every night. What a gem! Her parents don't know they're alive. Her father was a bloody nightmare when he was wee: felt like he never slept a whole night, ever. That's when you learn about sleep deprivation. No wonder they use it in interrogations. How did we ever survive with so little sleep and then off to work in the morning? Surprised I never crashed the car on the way there. The other two grandkids are fine though as well. I just never saw me buying one of them a pony!"

"Geez, maybe I should've brought my hat after all. That breeze is freezing. At least the snow has gone. Never lies for long these days. Global warming. Yet so many folk just don't believe it. It won't affect me of course. But poor Cordelia. What will the planet be like when she's my age? Right, which way? Up Blackness Road, Glamis Road and turn for home at the Spar (must get rolls) and what did Moira say? Toilet roll? No, kitchen roll, that's what it was. Or the usual, through the park and up to the Observatory? I haven't been up there for a couple of weeks to be fair, so let's do that. Funny how I associate that walk with Keane's "Hopes and Fears" album. A bit like thinking of John from the walking group every time I use shaving gel. Or that flat I had in Paris every time I smell Brut. I must've listened to that Keane album a hundred times on my walks through the park during lockdown. Not in the mood just now so let's just see what pops into my head."

"This bit up towards the bandstand is a lot steeper than you imagine. Feel how my breathing's heavier. But at least it's not like when it used to tighten up 10 years ago. That was scary. I really thought my heart was kaput. All those tests at Ninewells Hospital. Ectopic beat, eh? Hereditary as well! Wish Uncle Terry had mentioned it to me before I got myself in such a state. Grandad had it, he had it. And my dad probably had it too. But we wouldn't be in Spain so often now if it hadn't been for my panic. Every cloud and all that. I remember saying to Moira "I'd prefer to see Europe while I'm still alive!" And off we went. Just like that. She gets me does Moira."

"Those shouts above me are probably some football team or other training, running up the slope like we used to with the Kelso boys. Sounds like lots of encouragement from whoever's taking it. I loved that. Can't run anymore, though. But thank God I can still walk for miles. Looking forward to going back to Glencoe with my boys. The four Munros we're doing will take me up to about eighty in the bag. That's only slightly under a third of the total on the official list. Still, not bad for an old codger like me, eh? When is it again? End of June? Must check when I get back. Sure I wrote it on the calendar."

"Geez, look at that. A woman with five dogs. That's ridiculous! She must be a professional walker or something. Surely no-one would be daft enough to have five dogs of their own. Sometimes I honestly think I'm the only person in Balgay Park who doesn't have a dog. Nah, no chance of me having a dog! Mmm, she's nice. Hate those leggings though. Looks like she's walking around in her underwear. Thank God I never had a daughter. Oh, they've cleaned away all the fallen trees from the storm here. The path's clear again. Hey, that's from 'Somewhere only we know' off Keane's album. 'I came across a fallen tree, I felt the branches of it looking at me, Is this the place we used to love? Is this the place that I've been dreaming of?' It's ok. No-one can hear me. It's really quiet up here near the top. No-one's around."

"I'll do all three hills today. Up to the very top past the Observatory, down to the Balgay Bridge. Across then up to the Irish King's obelisk. Wonder if those trees on the corner at the top will be away now. Well, the bits that were blocking the path anyway. That storm didn't feel so awful watching it from the flat, but it obviously wreaked havoc here in the park. Still remember that crow following us up from the bridge, the day the snow came on. God, that was creepy. Moira was really spooked by it. Straight out of "The Omen". That was Easter Sunday too because we'd come to the park to roll our eggs. I can remember at least two Easter Sundays when it snowed in Dundee, including that one when everyone was in Camperdown Park and it suddenly turned into a blizzard. It was chaos! Cars stuck everywhere."

"Isn't this a great bridge? Everyone says it's haunted of course. We used to dare each other to cross it in the dark when we came to Lochee Park to see the fireworks on Bonfire night. Those displays were brilliant but I do recall having to leave one year because Greg was terrified of the noise. Pity the Council stopped the fireworks though. Much safer too. And now they've painted the bridge royal blue for some reason. Done the same to the bandstand. Actually looks pretty good, to be fair."

"Ah ha! I've got company. First people I've seen since I started up the hill. They look like a group of students. I wonder what language they're speaking. Up the pace, Jim boy! Oh, they're taking the wee shortcut I always take. They must know the paths. One lad and four girls, eh? Lucky boy! Nah, they're speaking English. Pity! I could've done with practising my French. I did a lot of walking when I was at St. Andrews because I was always broke. Student grant helped though. Went to the bank manager to ask for a £5 overdraft and got knocked back. Ended up busking."

"Third hill now. The smallest one. Not really a hill as such, More like a mound. Wonder if the plaques to all the bishops and canons have been fully repaired. Who was Canon Robertson again? Moira's great-uncle? Her grandad's brother. What does that make him? Never mind. Geez, it's so quiet up here now and the light's beginning to fade. Still got my radar though, just like I did on my way home from the dancing all those years ago. Never got jumped once. Probably thanks to keeping my wits about me and checking front and back. Must have crossed the street a million times just to avoid someone in the dark. Moira doesn't have any radar. That time in Pompeii when she wanted to check out that dark square at eleven o'clock at night, blissfully unaware of all those guys hanging around. Not a good idea. Same thing with that underpass in Central Park. Are you kidding? I've seen too many movies where it turns out really bad for anyone stupid enough to walk through. I'd like to go back to New York. It was cool but edgy at the same time."

"Oh, there's a newly-dug grave, ready for some poor bugger. Must be hard digging six feet down when the ground's so frozen. Jim, what are you saying? They use diggers these days, little JCBs. Would love to have a go on a JCB. Hey, it's getting quite dark now. Need to get a move on. Balgay Hill can be a bit creepy once the light goes. Look at that tall gravestone. Someone could easily be hiding there. What if a guy came out from behind it with a dog, a Rottweiler or something? What if he asked me the time? Would I keep walking and shout the time back to him? I definitely wouldn't stop, would I? You never know. But if his dog blocked my path, things could get serious. He'd probably have a weapon like a hammer in his hand. He'd come over, grab me and force me to my knees, yank off my backpack and make me hand over my wallet, phone and keys. That'd be my worst nightmare. But if I kept the head, I might survive. I could escape if I did exactly what he wanted. Or maybe he'd just leave now he had my stuff. Doubt it. I'd be so scared he'd hurt me. Or worse. He'd have the house keys. What if he found out where I lived from my phone or wallet? And then, just when I think he's going, he'd go behind me and "Whack!"

I'd waken up with a really sore head and earth on my face. He's buried me in that grave. I'd claw and claw and scream and scream but eventually give up and wait for the inevitable.

"Shit, Jim, ha! ha! Calm down and get a grip, will you? You've got the most outrageous imagination, honestly! Where does all that nonsense come from? Too many horror books when you were young. You're frightened of your own shadow, so you are. Nobody gets jumped on Balgay Hill, robbed then thrown in a grave. Buried alive! More

Keane. 'Bedshaped' "Many, the lives we lived in each day and buried altogether".

-Right, come on, let's get down the hill, go over by Mum's grave, say 'Hello' then up to the Spar for kitchen roll. If I go back down Blackness Road, I should make the kick-off in time. What time is it? Hmm, I'll be cutting it fine. Right, let's crack on. Have I got a beer to watch the game with? Think so. Hey, where did that big black dog come from? I fucking hate dogs! And this one doesn't look all that friendly. Shit!"

- Have you got the time, mate?

5
OBSERVATORY

It was the first item on the 6 o'clock STV news.

"Police Scotland Chief Inspector David Bailey has told reporters there has been no progress in finding the young Dundee boy who disappeared without trace from Balgay Park in the west of the city five days ago. Nine-year old Sam Gibson, who is autistic, had gone for a walk after school with his mother Claire but had wandered away from her as she sat on a park bench. Sam has not been seen since and there are no clues as to his whereabouts. The Police are anxious to trace the boy who takes regular medication to treat his type-1 diabetes. When last seen, he was wearing a navy-blue Superdry hoodie, grey school trousers and black Sketchers trainers. He is tall for his age, five foot nine, and has short red hair. Anyone with any information should contact Police Scotland or the local police in Dundee using the non-emergency 101 number."

Claire turned from the TV to look at her mum, who was once again quietly sobbing into a handkerchief. Both of them had experienced the harshest of emotions over the previous four days and today had not been any better. The pain was still as sharp as the day Sam had so mysteriously vanished into thin air and neither of them could find any words that might make things more bearable. They had expected some kind of news by now but the search had drawn a total blank. It appeared that Claire was the last person to see Sam before he disappeared from beside the bench she was sitting on. If only she hadn't been so wrapped up in that email she had been writing to her solicitor. He said it was urgent and that he needed her instruction before six that evening so he could present the custody appeal to the judge the next day. It wasn't like she was playing Spider Solitaire, was it? That email was very important for their futures. She had to keep Sam with her. God knows what would happen if he went to live with that pig of a father.

But now, the custody could wait. They had to find Sam first and hopefully discover why he went away. The court case had probably driven him to go and find some peace and quiet away from the wrangling and name-calling. But he had to be somewhere. He couldn't just not be around any more like that Lord Lucan guy. They'd checked all of his family and friends (Sam didn't have loads of friends), but he hadn't turned up at anybody's door to get a bed for the night, meaning he might be hiding somewhere they hadn't looked yet, or even sleeping rough. Thank God it was late August and the weather was still fairly warm. But what about his diabetes? If he has a hypo, he could easily fall unconscious and God knows what then. He wouldn't die, would he? Claire was unsure about the answer and made a mental note to find out.

After blowing her nose repeatedly, her mum finally broached the elephant in the room, the possibility that Sam had been abducted. But Claire was having none of it. She insisted that, for a big lad like Sam, ok autistic but sturdy all the same, and with his karate training, it was pretty unlikely that anyone could have physically forced him into a car or something. They all knew what a whirlwind Sam was when he went off on one, especially if he was being asked to do something he really didn't want to do. Admittedly, he could have been persuaded by someone to go somewhere, but Sam usually felt safer when he was close to her and didn't like being away for any length of time, so that just made it all the more puzzling why he'd gone.

Claire's mum asked her to go over the details of that evening yet again and reluctantly she agreed.

"Right mum, I've told you a hundred times, it was a perfectly normal school day and nothing untoward had happened. I picked him up at the school gate on Glenagnes Road, I asked him how his day had been and I suggested we have a walk around Balgay Park before tea. Sam seemed well happy with that and showed me the tennis ball he always had in his coat pocket, hinting that we could have a game of *Granny*, you know that's his favourite, once we got there. On the way up to the park, he told me about a new lady who had come to work with him in the section and how she'd been fascinated by the special things he could do, like juggling 3 balls, counting in his head and all that stuff he knows about space travel. She seemed quite impressed. I laughed when he said he'd told her he didn't like her perfume! Typical Sam, eh?"

At that, Claire was momentarily overwhelmed again and sat in floods of tears while her mum went to make a pot of tea for them. The two devastated women sipped their tea in silence, searching for the key that would unlock the puzzle and bring Sam back to them. Then Claire continued.

"When we reached the entrance to Balgay Park, Sam spent a moment or two patting a wee dog that had taken a fancy to him. All the dogs love him, don't they? That's the only point where anything unusual occurred. After the dog ran back to its owner, Sam just stood there, as if he was listening for something, or could hear something I couldn't. I had a listen too but there was nothing, honest. I asked him what it was but he didn't answer me. So I distracted him with the offer of a game of *Granny* over on the grass, not far from the first bench on the road through the park. He won of course like he always does. He's just so athletic. Then, after he'd lectured me again on how to improve my catching, he suddenly went back to listening again and turning round and round. You know how amazing they say his hearing is, so I just thought he could pick out a conversation or something. But that's when my phone pinged and it was the bloody solicitor asking for that information so I had to go and answer him. Sam came over to the bench as well and put his tennis ball down beside me. I wrote the email and when I looked up he was gone."

■ ■

Sam had had a good day at school and was desperate to tell his mum all about the new lady who had come to work with him. Although she had asked him an awful lot of questions, it had given him the chance to tell her all the things he knew he was good at. She liked his juggling, even though she was a total disaster at it herself, and she seemed genuinely interested in his explanation about the force it took to get a rocket off the ground. But she really smelled of rotten flowers or something, so he had told her he didn't like it. She might smell better tomorrow. With that in mind, he ran over to the gates where his mum was as usual waiting for him with his Pink Lady in her hand, gave her a big hug and a kiss on the cheek (twice in fact), took the apple from her, grabbed her hand and pulled her away down the hill.

When she asked how his day had been, Sam related enthusiastically his hour with the new lady, what he'd had for lunch and what Miss Barnett had told the Headmistress about Kelly-Lee. They were standing outside the door but he'd heard every word. He jumped at mum's suggestion of a walk in Balgay Park just up the hill and he was quick to remind her he still had his tennis-ball with him so they could have a game of *Granny*. That would be great because mum was hopeless at catching and he would win again as he always did. Only his dad had once beaten him but he'd cheated and Sam hated him for that, and for hitting his mum.

At the gates to the park, Sam played with a little dog that had come running over to him. His mum was busy telling the owner how all the dogs loved Sam and what a pity it was that they couldn't have their own dog because the landlord didn't allow it. And then, just as he stood up from petting the dog, he heard it. A new sound. He tried to fix on it more accurately but it kept coming and going. His natural curiosity insisted that he get closer, but mum wanted to play *Granny* and he couldn't resist his favourite game, so he took the ball from his pocket and mockingly ran over onto the grass, teasing mum with his ability to catch his own throws high up into the air. The game itself was entirely one-sided, Sam caught every one of his mum's pathetic throws and she was soon one letter away from defeat, resisting the urge to tell Sam not to throw the ball so brutally hard at her. That was Sam, it wasn't his fault. His next piledriver flew through her despairing hands and caught her on the chin, but Sam was too busy celebrating his latest victory to notice that mum had winced in pain. Once again, he ran over to explain to his mum what she would have to do to get better at catching, but in the middle of it, he stopped. There it was again. That noise. Where was it coming from? Wait, there were lots of sounds, all mixed up. Sam turned round several times to locate the source of the noise. It didn't seem to be coming from the park and it definitely wasn't from the roads nearby. Could it be coming from above him?

At that, his mum's phone pinged and she paused to read a message. She then suggested they go back over to the bench so she could answer, as it had to be done at once. But Sam wasn't listening to her: his attention was elsewhere. On auto-pilot, he walked over to the bench with his mum but didn't sit down beside her. He carefully placed his tennis-ball next to her and walked round behind the bench. Mum began to compose her answer, hunched over her phone and peering at the small screen, bemoaning the evening sunshine which made writing a text almost impossible. By now, Sam was certain the sounds were coming from up the hill so he quietly walked away from the bench, found the almost hidden stairs, skipped up the first few and disappeared out of sight.

■■

It took Sam less than three minutes to emerge onto the junction of the two roads that snake around Balgay Hill. Although the path up from the park was relatively steep, he had hardly noticed it, so fixed was he on finding the source of the increasingly loud noises he could hear in his head. He continued straight over and followed the road up and around to the right past the large chestnut tree his mum took him to each September to collect conkers. There hadn't been any sounds there in the past but now he could hear a complex series of beeps and trills with a background of almost constant white noise. Further up the slope and nearly at the top,

Sam hesitated momentarily to check if the noise might be coming from his right where the hill swept back down to his gran's house on Ancrum Drive. No, the source was definitely to his left in the direction of the Mills Observatory. He jogged on and up to the high point then stopped and listened. There was no longer any doubt. He'd found it. The noise was coming from inside the observatory.

As the location was clearly closed to the public at that hour, Sam went round to the left, ignoring the splendid panorama of the river Tay to the south, and placed both his hands on the wall. Yes, he knew he was right. He could feel the tingle of some kind of electrical power washing through the sandstone blocks of the building. The noise had now settled to a constant hum of electrical circuits and relays. Sam had no idea what could be running inside the observatory building to cause such a cacophony of sounds but he became more and more agitated, desperate to get inside and see what it might be. Having seen on his arrival that the entrance was both locked and shuttered, he continued round to the back of the building, checking to see if there was a window he could see through or even access. To his disappointment, all was secure.

Sam was beginning to get quite upset. He really didn't like being thwarted by anyone or anything when he was determined to do something, and he often found it difficult, if not impossible, not to rage against the total unfairness of things. He had to get in. By now he was at the north-facing wall where he spent some time examining a large drain cover and a round disc in the ground, but neither proved to be of any help to him. He sat down on the drain cover and stared at the building. Suddenly he heard what sounded like an electric gate opening and his eyes opened wide with excitement as, right in front of him, he watched the five bicycle racks he could see next to the wall begin to rise slowly into the air and click into place parallel with the ground.

-Come in, Sam. I'll show you around, said a friendly voice from below.

Being a boy who was rarely fearful of new things (unlike the others at school), Sam dashed over to the bike racks and saw that a staircase had opened up beneath them. And there was a man at the bottom beckoning him to come down and repeating his invitation. Without a moment's hesitation nor a thought to his mother, Sam descended the thirteen steps (he counted them) and followed the man through a heavy metal door into a small room. The door closed behind him, as did the bike racks, unseen above.

-Well, you're a curious boy, aren't you? said the man. No stopping you, was there? Never mind, I'm sure you'll fit in, just like the other one did. I'm Mister McKay by the way, I run the observatory. Or at least, the bit the public get to see. Oh I nearly forgot. Here's a new tennis-ball for your pocket.

You left your old one down on the park bench. So, now that you're here, I'm sure you'd like to ask me a question or two.

Sam of course had a million questions in his head but, above all, he absolutely wanted to know if his suspicions were correct.

-This isn't just an observatory, is it? he asked.

-Oh you're sharp alright. Well, yes and no. I suppose it is a normal, functioning observatory to those outside and to anyone who visits. But yes, you're right. It's more than that. Much more than that. It took us a long time to persuade the authorities to build the observatory but we needed to get our reports sent out with the minimum of fuss. And you're in luck. Today is report day. That's what you've been hearing. The other boy was special too and could hear the signal going out as well. But that was quite a while ago. Would you like to meet him?

-Of course I would, replied Sam, having completely forgotten about the world he'd left down the hill in

Balgay Park. Mister McKay led Sam to a lift which took them down to a new level. When the door slid open, Sam followed the man through a sort of umbilical tube and then through a second door which also slid open as they approached. Sam gasped. There before him was the interior of a huge spacecraft with lights and screens blinking frantically to the same rhythms he had heard outside. The source. As he looked around in disbelief mixed with real excitement, a young boy approached.

-Ah, John, said Mister McKay. You'll be delighted to know you'll have a friend from now on. This is Sam. Sam, this is John. He came to us in a similar way to you. It caused a lot of fuss out there but John's happy here and does some great work for us. He'll show you the ropes once the signal's been sent through the telescope and we shut down again. You two boys are going to save me a lot of the energy I use looking like this. It often exhausts me, pretending to be a human when the observatory's open. However, at the rate this planet's going, we'll only have about twenty more reports to send and it'll be time to leave. Before it burns.

-Is that what you're doing? Sam queried. You're monitoring the climate change here. Do you know how long you've been here?

-The assimilation programme puts it at one thousand five hundred of your years, Sam. When we landed and penetrated the hill, there weren't many people around. And we covered our presence pretty well I think. We had very little to report until your industrial revolution. Then it all took off you might say.

At that, John interrupted to say the report had finished sending.

-Shall I shut down, Mister McKay? Then Sam and I can chat before it's time for the sleeping pods. Yes? OK, come on, Sam. I'll show you the rest of the place. There's loads to see and you won't believe what all the buttons can do.

Sam hesitated slightly, unsure of what to say next. Mister McKay was frank.

-I'm going back up to open the observatory, boys. And yes, Sam. You're right. You'll be staying here. You won't be going back home.

Sam smiled and shrugged his shoulders. He wanted to stay. It would be fun.

****

As Mister McKay was unlocking the shutter on the observatory entrance, a woman ran up to him. She was upset and crying. In her hand was a tennis-ball.

-Excuse me, she said. Have you seen my boy? He's about your height with ginger hair.

-Sorry, love, came the reply. I haven't seen a soul all day.

6
BRIDGE

It was in the middle of her normal walk with Bailey her cockapoo that Alison blundered on the portal. Of course, at the time, she had no idea there was a portal. She had been crossing the Balgay Bridge from the Observatory side to the cemetery side to and fro every day for years, and her thoughts tended to be restricted to what a lovely place it was and how daft all the myths and tales about it being haunted were. She had never "felt" anything untoward nor heard any noises other than the wind in the trees and the distant traffic on Glamis Road.

But it was different that Wednesday morning in 2014. She came down the old steps from the Observatory as usual, keeping Bailey on about two metres of lead so there was no risk of a trip, and turned right at the bottom of the slope on to the blue bridge. At that point, Bailey started to bark, apparently at something already on the bridge. But it was empty. Alison frowned and told the dog to be quiet. And with the barking gone, she was aware of a faint buzzing noise coming from somewhere ahead of her, which she took to be perhaps bees or wasps. She chose to remain where she was.

Now, like most people, Alison was less than happy at the thought of hundreds of wasps blocking her path. In fact, having two or three of the horrible things in her way would have had the same effect on her. She resolved to stay where she was until the buzzing went away, not wanting to risk an attack on herself or her pet. The more she stared however, the more certain she became that there were no insects flying around the bridge, other than the odd midge a few feet in front of her. So, despite the continued sound of a high-pitched buzzing, she told herself that all was well and made to cross. But Bailey was unusually reluctant to follow her, so Alison had to go back, pick up the fearful dog and carry him over the bridge.

Halfway across, Bailey squealed and leapt from her arms in a vain attempt to run back to the Observatory side, but Alison reined him back with the telescopic lead and started to give him a real talking-to about settling down and behaving like he'd been taught to. In mid-sentence, she suddenly sensed a strange quivering in her bones, which, coupled with the buzzing, left her feeling slightly nauseous and ill at ease. But, at her age, this was quite a frequent occurrence. She told herself it was time to move on and finish the walk. She shivered as if the temperature had fallen by a couple of degrees as she passed the midpoint then quickened her pace and crossed the bridge.

At the cemetery end, she noted that Bailey was now his normal self again and was pulling at his lead to move on up the slope to the southern viewpoint over the river Tay. Alison suddenly noticed that the buzzing had stopped and everything seemed perfectly calm and normal again, so she allowed Bailey to pull her up the slope where she stopped to take in the panorama. She loved that view so much. There before her lay the great expanse of the river Tay, one and a half miles wide at the mouth but narrowing quickly to the west of the famous railway bridge that took trains south to the Kingdom of Fife and beyond. Alison smiled to herself as she sat down on the park bench a few yards from the corner and searched in her backpack for the metal bowl and bottle of water which allowed her to keep Bailey hydrated on their walks. The dog responded with his usual enthusiasm and whined gently as his owner prepared the drink which he proceeded to lap up noisily.

As Alison bit into the Snickers bar she'd brought as a snack, she noticed a newspaper below the bench. It was the local Dundee Courier. For no particular reason, she stooped down and picked it up. Turning it to the front page, she was surprised to see that there was no news to be read, but simply a full page of classified adverts and announcements. That reminded her of the old Couriers of her parents' time. She glanced at the date. June 2 1964. How very strange! That was exactly 50 years ago to the day, yet the newspaper appeared to have been freshly printed. Who could have had such an old paper up on the hill and decided to just throw it away? Why, it might even be a collectors' item, or a copy from the day someone had been born, like you find in some shops. Alison's instincts were to leave the paper on the bench where its owner could retrieve it if they so wished, should they return.

And indeed, at that very moment, an old gentleman approached from one of the smaller paths and smiled broadly as he got closer to a now slightly bemused Alison.

-Ah! There it is. My paper. It must have fallen from under my arm as I walked by here a few minutes ago. Did you find it on the path? No matter, I have it now. God knows the trouble I'd be in had I gone back home with the milk and rolls but no Courier. I would've been sent straight back out to get another one. Well, I'd best be off. Enjoy the view and thank you.

Alison had no opportunity to ask the obvious questions flying around inside her head before the gentleman set off down the hill towards the bridge. What the heck was going on? It was time to head back and figure out what this had all been about. She packed away the water bowl, stood up, pulled Bailey to attention and set off after the man, glancing one last time at the estuary below her feet. Wait a minute! She rubbed her eyes and looked again. Where the hell was the road bridge? No, it must be a trick of the light. That's impossible! And where the bridge should have been, Alison could make out two small boats passing each other in the middle of the river. Some kind of tug boats? Instinctively she pulled her mobile phone from her pocket and made to capture the scene on camera, but the phone was completely dead. She then shook herself to try and chase away the weird images she was seeing, before heading quickly down the path to the blue bridge. Except it wasn't blue anymore!

"This is getting silly!" Alison silently scolded herself as she crossed the bridge, ignoring the strange shivers and the buzzing and the lack of colour, pausing only when both she and the whining and fearful Bailey were safely on the Observatory side again.

She stopped at the end and turned to look back across.

"Ach! The bridge IS blue. Of course it's blue. How could it be otherwise? This bloody menopause is playing havoc with my sanity, she said to herself. Come on Bailey. Let's get back to the flat. I need a strong coffee."

As strange as this incident had been, it did not put Alison (or Bailey) off including the bridge in their daily walks, mainly because it was a regular habit and nothing remotely similar occurred again. Until the 11 July that is, when the buzzing returned just as she set foot on the blue bridge. Alison hesitated long enough to double-check for bees or wasps, her eyes quickly scanning the length of the bridge, but her attention was dragged back to her dog who had started barking again and was pulling her back towards the Observatory. So once again Bailey had to be picked up and carried across. Alison recognised the shivers and nausea as she passed the midpoint but remained calm and proceeded to the cemetery side where she put down a much calmer Bailey and turned left up the slope.

As she walked uphill, she was aware that this part seemed less crowded with old headstones than before and even the trees appeared smaller. But the huge memorial to the Ballantyne family at the top on the corner reassured her that the cemetery probably was as it usually was. However, she started to think back to the previous incident, wondering if there could be any connection between what had happened then and what she was feeling now. She began to imagine that there would be a Courier under the bench at the top.

Alison wasn't at all disappointed to discover that there was no such thing: no Courier. And no bench! She checked the estuary, perturbed initially by how difficult it was to see through the clouds of dense smoke hanging over the town. Was the road bridge there? She was unsure but it didn't seem to be. And where had all those dozens of chimneys come from? It was like a real scene from a photo of Dundee when it was Juteopolis. Factories and chimneys and smoke.

Alison was pulled from her reverie by the approach of a young man dressed in Highland military uniform, similar to a painting she still had of her Grandad Joe aged 18 in the Black Watch. The man stopped a couple of paces away.

"Good morning, missus. What a cute wee dog. But I haven't seen one like that before. Is it a new breed?"

Alison could only nod. The soldier continued:

"Lovely today isn't it? And what a grand day too for the royal visit. Are you going into town to see them? It says in the Courier they're going to officially open the construction of the new concert hall. Just imagine, King George and Queen Mary actually in Dundee. That should be something to cheer us all up what with all this talk of war. There's also a list of where they'll be at different times. Would you like to see?"

The young soldier stretched open his newspaper so Alison could read inside. She was close to panicking but said thank you and leaned towards the paper a little and pretended to read the timetable. But her eyes arrowed directly towards the date at the top of the page. She let out a gasp and staggered back, hand to her mouth. The soldier dropped his paper and attempted to steady the swooning woman.

"My God, are you ok, missus? What's wrong? Did you have a dizzy turn?"

Alison did her best to regain her composure but found it difficult to speak.

"Yes…. Oh!.. No! Thank you. I'm just a little… I must…. get back…. back home."

With that, Alison pulled Bailey away from the soldier and back down the slope to the bridge. She paused before crossing over.

"Did that Courier really say 11 July 1914? 100 years ago? How could that be? What the hell is happening to me? Am I mad?"

She made to cross but the dog held back, whimpering loudly.

"Come on, Bailey. I don't need this, you know. I'm losing my mind and you're frightened of a bit of buzzing. Now do what you're told and let's get home."

Bailey however was having none of it and seemed genuinely terrified of crossing the bridge. Alison tugged on his lead to no avail.

"Bailey, I swear, I'll leave you here if I have to. Come on!"

But eventually Alison gave in, picked up her pet and walked across the bridge, not even registering the colour of its paint. She passed the midpoint with a shiver and some rapid blinking of her eyes but, despite Bailey's squirming in her arms, she continued over the bridge, down the nearest path and onto the park road which led back to her flat in Scott Street. Safely inside, Alison fed the dog, made a cup of tea, and sat at the living-room window, staring out towards the city. She then got up and took a notepad from the top drawer of her sideboard, and scribbled down some calculations based on the dates of the two strange incidents.

"So how can I appear to have travelled back fifty years in time the first day I heard the buzzing and now today 100 years? This is madness. I'm going insane. I must be. I'll need to go to the library to check a visit to Dundee by ... which King and Queen was it? George and Elizabeth? No, Mary, it was Mary. Time travel is impossible they say. If I'm not mad then it has to be the menopause but that's ridiculous. I've never heard of any woman having that kind of hallucinations. What will the doctor say? She won't believe me. She'll put me on triazolam again. No, not that. I was like a zombie the last time. I have to do this myself. It feels so very real. Could it be true? Did I actually go back in time? Maybe I could prove it by doing it again, only taking pictures this time. Yes, they'd have to believe me then. I'll take my ancient Kodak camera with me on my walks with Bailey from now on. Right, that's what I'll do. But in the meantime, I'll say nothing to anyone."

And so Alison didn't go back to the doctor's. She just made a point of having her old camera in her bag each time she and Bailey went out. She also spent an hour or so in Blackness library where she was able to confirm there had indeed been a royal visit to Dundee by King George V and Queen Mary on 10 July 1914 only weeks before the outbreak of World War I. During their visit, the royal couple had laid the foundation stone of what would become the Caird Hall. The young soldier had been telling her the truth! This helped convince Alison that she wasn't mad at all but had somehow found some kind of "door" that led to the past. She hardened her resolve to prove this with a photo and giggled at the thought of maybe becoming famous. She calculated that, if the pattern was repeated, then the next time she went through, she would be taken back 150 years to 1864 which meant she'd be able to take a photo of the Tay with no rail bridge either. What a scoop that would be!

In early December, Alison took Bailey for his morning constitutional up to the Observatory then down to the Balgay Bridge. As soon as she made to cross, the dog started to bark loudly and pull hard on his lead to go back. Alison's senses sharpened at once. Was today the day? She listened. Yes, there was a high-pitched buzzing coming from the middle of the bridge. The "door" was open again. She checked in her bag for her camera, confirmed there was a spool loaded inside, put an extra spool she'd bought online in her pocket and half-dragged Bailey towards the middle point where she momentarily hesitated and turned to the dog.

"Come on scaredy cat, I'm going to make us rich and you'll be the best-fed dog in Dundee."

At that, Alison stepped through the portal…. And plunged the 40 feet to the path below! Bailey watched her disappear through the "door" and felt the tension on his lead release. He sat down next to the plaque and waited for Alison to return.

Had the dog been able to read, he would have seen that the Balgay Grounds were opened in 1871.

The bridge was constructed the following year.

LAST DAY

-Dave! Dave! Dave! Wake up! Dave, wake up!

Dave resisted the call to awaken from his slumber, but the shock of hearing his dad's voice after all those years made him open his eyes wide, look to his right and scream. Naturally I'd turned off his volume as I always do, just in case. He screamed again.

-It's OK, Dave. Everything's going to be just fine. But we have so much to do. It's already half past seven. We need to get cracking. You don't want to waste your last day now, do you?

-Dad? You are my Dad, right? My Dad who died twenty-odd years ago? Last day? What do you mean?

-Yes, Dave. I'm sorry to say, your time is now. You die today.

Dave let out another scream then burst into tears. He made to get up out of bed but couldn't manage somehow. I had to keep him there until I'd explained everything.

-This is the normal routine, Dave, for someone who's behaved him or herself. A family member, in this case *me*, comes back to help you have a final fling before you die. A kind of going-away party that only they know about. And as I'm a bit of an expert on my only son's likes and dislikes, I've a few suggestions for you. That's better: you seem to be calming down. Now firstly, how would you like to make love to your wife Margaret for a final time?

-What? I don't believe this. I'm still asleep and I'm dreaming. You're not here Dad. I'd love you to be, but that can't be. You're dead.

-Of course I'm dead Dave. You helped lower me into my grave at Balgay cemetery twenty-six years ago last May. Yes, I've been dead ever since, but I've been sent back to make your passing as smooth as possible. It happens to everybody. So, back to business, would you like to get your leg over just one more time?

-Dad, if you are who you say you are. God I can't believe I'm having a conversation about me dying with my dead father. Dad, if you know all about me, you know that even if I wanted to, I probably couldn't......

-Don't worry, Dave. Margaret will do all the work. And you'll be surprised what an effect that'll have on you. Here she is, she's wakening up too. I'll wait in the kitchen.

"Most of the men I have to visit accept the chance to have a last romp in bed and I've learned to go into another room and wait patiently, trying hard not to listen to what is going on obviously. Even if I'm not really his Dad except for today, I still don't fancy thinking back to what was for me one of life's great pleasures. Not now. But I have to admit that those on their last day tend to ask for it at some point so I thought I'd just suggest it to Dave while he was already in bed with his wife. Oh! It sounds like Margaret has started to work her old magic on the man she thought had lost his mojo a long time ago. She'll enjoy it too. Just as well, as she'll have a fair bit of crying to do before the day's out. Poor soul! Ah-ha! I can hear the shower now and, with a bit of luck they're both in there now. Well done you two!"

At that, Dave came through into the kitchen with a look of utter incredulity on his face. I knew he was incredulous on both counts: me being here and the performance he'd just given in the bedroom. I congratulated him on the latter and suggested he have that full Scottish he normally only got on his birthday.

-As much as I'd love to, Dad, there's only muesli and prunes for breakfast this morning.

-Check the fridge, son!

Picking up on how the day might be panning out, Dave strode over to the fridge, opened the door wide, gave me a slightly troubled grin and bend down. I heard him gasp. When he came back up, he had a plate piled high with eggs, bacon, sausages, Stornoway black pudding, fried bread, beans and mushrooms.

-Two minutes in the microwave should see that about perfect, Dave.

-The microwave's broken, Dad.

-Not today it's not!

Two and a half minutes later, Dave was tucking into the best breakfast he'd ever had or so it seemed. In between mouthfuls, he asked me dozens of questions, all designed to reassure himself that this was not in fact his last day at all but just some miraculous visit from his long-lost Dad. It would have been easy for me to let him think that, but then I wouldn't have been doing my job which was to get clients ready to pass, even if they all resisted in some form or other. I didn't of course tell him where and when the moment would come, as that would just bring on an avalanche of avoidance ploys like not going near water, looking umpteen times before crossing the road, not taking the lift, giving big dogs a wide berth and definitely not driving a car. None of that works of course and they all die exactly like they're meant to, but you should see the lengths they'll go to just to get another few minutes on this mortal coil.

-Did you enjoy that, Dave?

-Dad, that was fantastic! I feel far too good for this to be my end.

-Sorry, son, it absolutely has to be. But don't fret, you've got a game of tennis with Gordon to play at twelve, and I think you might have a chance today.

-Do you think so? I haven't been hitting the ball so well lately. Still rarely get my first serve in after 30 years of trying. Any tips? Maybe I should stick to baseline rallies.

-Sure, if you think that'll work. Just remember it's your last game ever and you need to relax. And everyone who's played tennis knows that the more you relax, the better you play.

-I hope so. I'd love to put one over on that big-headed Gordon. He beat me in straight sets last week and I think I only won five games the whole match. Wait a minute; it's not going to happen on the Balgay courts, is it?

--Not allowed to say, my boy. You'll see. I wouldn't hide under that tree behind the courts if there's thunder and lightning though! Remember, it's made of metal. Only joking, son. Only joking.

So Dave went off to the tennis courts on Balgay Road for his weekly game with his old University pal. He was incredibly careful crossing the road, and made a point of not walking under any trees. He even checked the path through the park for runaway bicycles and misdirected Frisbees, before going to meet Gordon who was already practising his serve. I of course knew he still didn't believe entirely in what I'd told him. He probably dismissed the tumble in the sheets and the full English as something he'd dreamed, which was quite a denial and a huge stretch of the imagination, but most people find dying a bit difficult to accept, especially when they feel as well as he did.

Once on court, Dave won the toss of the coin to serve first. He settled down, tossed the ball high in the air and gave it all he had. Gordon didn't even move as the ball bounced in and accelerated past him. An ace. 15-love. Three serves later, it was 1-0 and Gordon still hadn't touched the ball. Dave had served four straight aces! Now it was his turn to receive and he knew how seldom he managed to return even Gordon's second serves when he was having a good day. His opponent slammed in his first serve, Dave stuck out his racket to the right, and to his utter amazement the ball flew back across the net, caught the baseline and crashed into the safety fence behind. Love-15! Dave began to think that maybe, just maybe, I was actually there helping him win and that this was really happening. But because he wasn't concentrating, Gordon's next serve beat him all ends up. 15-all.

-Dave, son, I whispered in his ear. Stop thinking about what I've told you this morning. Just play tennis.

Dave looked around, but I was nowhere to be seen. So he did what I'd told him to do and within the hour had put his pal to the sword 6-1, 6-2, 6-1. What a win! More a walkover! Gordon came to the net to shake hands with him and his face showed he could hardly believe he'd been thrashed so easily by someone he beat week in, week out. Dave could hardly contain himself but settled for a humble "Luck was on my side today" to explain his sudden spike in form.

Strangely though, after the tennis match, every time Dave tried to talk to Gordon about what had happened to him that morning, something else came out. That was my doing. I couldn't let him give the game away now, could I? That included Margaret who was still in bed sleeping like a baby next to the only man she'd ever loved.

I made sure both players decided to have a couple of pints in the Balgay Bar down Blackness Road, as they often did post-tennis. In between pints, Dave, sensing a moment again, tried his luck on the one-armed bandit. I let him win a couple of quid but we had bigger fish to fry, so I persuaded him not to take a lift home in Gordon's car, not being able to guarantee him a happy outcome. He was only too willing to agree with my suggestion. We walked slowly back up the hill towards his flat, talking about his life and his successes. No regrets were expressed by either of us and I got the impression he was going to have a fairly happy death. I tried to make him comfortable with the idea that being dead is in fact relatively pleasant as nothing ever goes wrong once you're dead. You have definitely passed the worst bit! As usual I didn't manage to totally persuade my client that it was all for the best, but I like to think I allayed most of his fears.

-You know, Dad, today has gone so well and I feel so lucky that I'm going to break the habit of a lifetime and buy a scratch card at the shop on the corner.

-Up to you, son. You never know.

The script was perfect. It was getting on for teatime. The evening paper told him his favourite team, Dundee, had won that day's derby against Dundee United by four goals to nil, Dave bought a Cadbury's Dairy Milk to celebrate, and when he scratched his Lucky Sevens card, I made sure he got a prize of £77,777. And that's what gave him the heart attack!

Dave lay in bed next to Margaret, feeling the pain increase in his upper chest and left arm and unable to get any sort of sound out of his throat except a low moan. He glanced at the clock on the wall. It was seven-thirty in the morning. Dave closed his eyes for the last time. I helped him up and we both stood at the bedside looking down on his body. Margaret was still asleep.

-There. That wasn't so bad now, was it Dave?

-Actually it was ok really. Especially the tennis. Wait a minute, where's my Dad?

-He's with the others Dave. I just became him to help not scare you. Sometimes I have to be someone's Mum, or even their Gran. Well, we'll leave it to Margaret to get on with things now. She'll wake up in about an hour. She'll be fine though. You know that. I have my next appointment soon and I'm allowed to invite you to come along and see how things work out if you'd like. No-one will see or hear you of course. But if you prefer, you can just go and meet the others.

They're all there: your Mum, both your Grans and Grandads. And your Dad of course!

8

OUCH TREE

Gavin had just about everything he'd ever wanted. Aged 16 and doing Highers at the only fee-paying school in Dundee, his life was a constant reminder of how wealthy his parents were. Big house on Blackness Avenue, two Audis, an electric scooter for him, designer clothes and shoes, electric and acoustic guitars, a Clavinova, an entertainments room with every game module available linked to a 100-inch wall-mounted screen, a 10-metre swimming pool under glass at the back of the house, and four holidays a year including with friends. He was tall, handsome, sporty, clever, witty and not even a blowhard like some of his similarly-rich mates. What better start in life could a boy have?

Sarah. Sarah Bentley. She would have made his life better than it was. That's what he would think every single day at school, and afterwards with his mates in their homes or in Balgay Park up the road where they drank and vaped in the old bowling green most evenings. Yeah! Life was good and he was having a ball. But she would have made it perfect. If there was really such a thing as love at first sight then that's what had happened that start of third year when she walked into the register class, the new girl from another town. Gavin couldn't take his eyes off her and made a point of sitting close to her in the subjects they shared. As soon as he knew she was taking Physics, he went to his guidance teacher and said he no longer felt

German was right for him and he wished to be enrolled in the Physics class. And with his parents' backing of course, he got the change he wanted.

It was taking him much longer than he expected however to pluck up the courage to ask her out on her own, despite being in her company dozens of times at weekend parties and making sure she became a member of the crowd he ran with. This meant he had plenty opportunity to get to know her better over the course of his third year, her likes and dislikes in sport, music and fashion, what it had been like in Edinburgh before her family moved to accommodate her father's job at Ninewells Hospital. She even came round to tea at his house a couple of times but she was always with her friend Kathleen on these occasions, so the chance to move their relationship on rarely presented itself.

Sarah really liked Gavin. He was great fun to be around and always seemed to be the centre of attention when all the friends gathered somewhere, especially if he started to play guitar or piano. He was clearly musically talented and she liked how he was so humble about his ability on the keyboard in particular. Most of the other boys had somewhat inflated ideas about themselves. But not Davie. No, Davie was just perfect. Another tall, handsome and clever boy, but with a wonderful personality that set him apart from all the others. His talent at football did no harm to his image either, as he was the only one in his year-group who had already signed schoolboy forms with a professional football club. Sarah had felt a flutter in her heart the first time she'd met him and had decided from early on to nurture an increasingly-cosy relationship with him, slow, subtle and very deliberate. She liked Gavin too, but she was convinced she was in love with Davie. He might even be the one.

After months and months of uncertainty and prevarication, Gavin made his move at the fourth year Christmas disco in the school, dancing with the group of girls which included Sarah and joining in the conversations between songs. Late on, when a slow tune was played and the floor emptied a little, he grabbed Sarah's hand and pulled her into the centre, slipping his arms around her waist and gently pulling her in. She responded by happily draping her arms around his neck and whispering into his ear. But it was not about them. In fact it was about basically everyone else in S4 except them. How Kathleen had told her that Christine was going to chuck Ethan because Paul had suggested they get together and she quite fancied that. And lots more!

Gavin was raging inside. And in his rage, he lost his patience. He suddenly brought his face up from the nape of Sarah's neck and planted his lips firmly on hers, trying to push his tongue into her mouth. It was a disaster. Sarah recoiled and asked him what he was doing. Was he drunk? Why did he try to kiss her without asking first? Gavin couldn't find the words to explain what he'd done, so, with a rapidly reddening face, hurried off the dance floor, found his jacket and went home. He was devastated. What he didn't realise was that, despite the shock, Sarah wasn't all that upset and just assumed Gavin had somehow got his emotions all twisted, and had confused friendship with more than that.

Being such a level-headed young lady, Sarah resolved to talk the incident through with Gavin and try to persuade him that they were good friends but that was as far as it went. It didn't work. Gavin poured out his heart to her, swore undying love and suggested that she would slowly grow to love him the way he already loved her. Sarah insisted that that was unlikely to happen, but she diplomatically didn't mention how she felt about Davie in case that caused trouble in the group. Things were progressing well with the object of her affections and she had no intention of letting anything spoil that. Somehow, she managed to placate Gavin for the moment and guaranteed their friendship would continue. But absolutely no more tongues!

Yet here they were at the start of fifth year and Gavin could not get her out of his head. He tried again, more than once, after the Christmas disco fiasco, but the whole of his fourth year was spent vainly attempting to persuade Sarah to be his girlfriend. What made it worse was she didn't appear to already have a boyfriend or to be particularly interested in any one of the lads from their group. And if she had someone from another school, no-one had ever seen him. He just couldn't understand what was wrong with him. And that made him sad. Despite all his home comforts, deep down he was sad to the point of hurting. The thing he wanted most was the thing he couldn't have.

One Friday evening in late October, just after the schools had gone back after the autumn break, Gavin got a call from one of his exes. She told him she'd been to Cineworld with her boyfriend the previous evening and guess who had been sitting in front of them. Sarah Bentley. With Davie! And they were definitely not just friends. The news broke Gavin's heart. He excused himself and hung up. How could she? Why Davie and not him? Feeling totally overwhelmed, he ran out of the house in a boiling rage and soon found himself sitting on a bench on the little roundabout at the entrance to Balgay Park. He slumped forward with his head in his hands and battled to hold back the tears welling up inside.

Suddenly there was a dishevelled old lady in a long black dress in front of him.

-Oh, look at you. Girl problems, eh? And it hurts so much!

-What would you know? Gavin hissed. A black cat at the woman's feet hissed back.

-I can help you, you know. With Sarah, I mean.

Gavin immediately leapt to his feet, towering over her up close.

-What the fuck do you know about Sarah and me, you old bag? Piss off and take a shower. You stink!

The old woman took a step back, unphased by Gavin's aggression.

-So you don't want her to be your girl anymore?

-Of course I do! Wait. What the fuck! How do you know about us?

-I read about lots of things, young man. In my teacup.

-Oh, I might have known. I come out to the park for some peace and quiet and along comes the local nutcase. Just my luck. Go on, piss off and leave me alone. I'm not in the mood.

-As you will, the old woman replied with a smile. But don't blame me if she marries Davie and lives happily ever after. Probably have a whole football team of kids.

-Shit! You know about Davie as well. What are you? Who are you? Why are you telling me all this?

- My name is Araucaria, she answered. I'm just an old lady who reads things in teacups, my dear boy. Anyway, you should remember me. You and your friends used to throw stones at my windows in

Jedburgh Road, shout terrible things about me on the street in front of my house and put unspeakable objects through my letter-box. You were very naughty in those days.

Gavin blushed slightly as he recalled the things he and his pals had gotten up to some years earlier. He mumbled an apology but mainly blamed the others. The old woman smiled and continued:

-I'll show you Sarah if you want. She's in the bowling-green waiting for you.

Gavin was off like a shot, racing round the 3-metre hedge on Blackness Road and leaping over the metal gate. Meanwhile the black cat slunk under the hedge and waited for him in the middle of the manicured grass. When Gavin heard Sarah call his name, he rushed over to where she was standing and then just stood, unable to believe his eyes. Sarah stretched out her arms and invited an embrace which he accepted at once, stepping forward and wrapping his arms tightly around...... nothing.

-What the ....! Sarah! Sarah! Where are you? Come back!

-She's gone.

Gavin spun round and the old woman was standing there, not two metres away, stroking the black cat in her arms.

-How did you get in here? Did you see where Sarah went? She just…. vanished!

-That wasn't Sarah, Gavin. That was a trick, to let you see what I can do. And I can do lots more…….. for a price. You can have Sarah for real if you want. If you have the nerve.

-How much will it cost me? Gavin said, emboldened by the knowledge that money was no object in his family.

-Just a bit of pain, Gavin, a wee bit of pain. That's all. I can replace the ache in your heart with another pain. A straight trade-off really. Come and I'll show you how to pay. It's just over there.

Araucaria led Gavin through the hedge at the rear of the tennis-courts and out onto the park itself.

She walked with him over towards Jedburgh Road and stopped next to two small monkey-puzzle trees.

-This is where you pay, Gavin. I call them the ouch-trees. It's quite simple really. Every day you have with Sarah is paid for by a certain amount of contact with those nasty little spikes you see there. Go on, touch one. It's not as bad as it looks and it's certainly worth it to get the girl of your dreams.

Gavin refused the invitation to touch the spikes. He thought they looked really vicious.

-Can I not just pay you money? he asked.

-No, dear, I'm sorry. The potion is free. But the spell is paid for with the pain which then triggers the potion. If you do that, Sarah will be all yours for a day.

-A day? That's not fair, is it? I want her forever. I love her.

-Let's start with just one day, so you can see what it'll be like. And you can of course stop any time you want. If you're serious, meet me here tomorrow night at eleven and bring me something from her: a piece of nail, an eyelash or just a single hair. I need it for the potion. And something from yourself too.

Gavin shrugged then stretched out his hand and laid it gently on one of the low branches. He could immediately feel the spikes against his skin, even with no pressure applied. He turned around to ask how long he would have to hold the branch, but Araucaria and her cat had gone.

Despite knowing how ridiculous all of this was, and believing it to be some kind of dream or hallucination, Gavin spent a sleepless night deciding whether to go through with the arrangement or not. His brain told him the whole thing was crazy, but the thrill he'd had when Sarah (or whatever that was) had welcomed him with open arms in the bowling green kept trumping his logical arguments and telling him to go back to the old woman.

The following day at school, he had little trouble getting a hair from the brush in Sarah's bag during their Physics lesson when she went to the loo and, at eleven that night, armed with her single hair and one of his own, he returned to the park where he found Araucaria waiting for him at the monkey-puzzle trees with a phial of liquid in her hand. Her black cat meowed as he approached. The old woman congratulated him on making a wise decision, invited him to push the two hairs into the phial, shook the liquid vigorously then opened it again and removed the hairs.

-There we are. The potion is ready, she said. It's as simple as that. Now to the payment. Are you ready?

Gavin nodded then grimaced as Araucaria took his hand and brought it over to one of the branches. He prepared himself.

-One last thing, Gavin, my dear. The ouch-tree does not like loud noises, so no screaming. Now, close your hand around the branch and squeeze.

Remember, if you do this, Sarah will be yours tomorrow. Go on, do it for the both of you.

Gavin took a deep breath and closed his left hand around the spiky branch. The pain was instant and sharp as the spikes stabbed his hand in a hundred places but he clenched his teeth and kept it there. Trails of blood dripped from his wrist.

-How… long… do I… keep it there? he managed to spit out despite the agony he was in.

-Oh that's quite enough, the old woman giggled. You can let go.

Gavin wrenched his hand back from the branch and cradled it tightly against his stomach, unable to hold back the tears. Araucaria continued:

-Well done my boy! You did it. Now all you have to do is get Sarah to drink some of the liquid in the phial and she'll be yours in minutes. 100% guaranteed.

And she was telling the truth. Despite a bandaged hand, Gavin managed to slip the liquid into Sarah's water-bottle during school lunches, she drank from it unaware of the extra special content and when Kathleen came to tell her Davie was waiting for her down at McDonald's, she told her to say she was busy with an assignment. Turning to Gavin, she smiled lovingly and continued:

-Gav, I think I've made a mistake about Davie. Can you ever forgive me? Let's get out of here. I can't face this afternoon's classes.

Gavin could hardly believe his ears and was a bit surprised when Sarah extended her hand to him. But he took it without hesitation and they left the school together via one of the side doors. As soon as they were alone, Sarah grabbed him tightly and kissed him softly on the lips. Gavin responded in kind and they were still kissing when they heard the bell summon the students back to class. But not for them. The two truants spent a blissful afternoon on the Dundee Law before going back to Gavin's for tea in his room. Sarah took no calls or messages from Davie that evening, and when she left for home, her eyes were still sparkling with happiness. After a last kiss, she promised Gavin she would dream of him that night in bed and told him to take care of the hand he'd scalded with the kettle.

Ecstatic, Gavin crawled off to his own bed, his head full of how amazing his afternoon and evening with Sarah had been. At last, she loved him! However, it was he who dreamed about her and not vice-versa. From midnight onwards, Sarah lay awake wondering what the hell she had just done and how she was going to get back with Davie. What had she been thinking? She and Gavin were friends but they would never be a couple.

The following day at school, Gavin greeted Sarah with a smile and a hug, neither of which she welcomed and he quickly surmised that the potion had worn off, so he played it cool and kept his thoughts to himself. Sarah managed to persuade Davie that she'd only helped Gavin home after he complained of being unwell and lied that her phone had run out of battery. Davie was initially unwilling to believe her story, but, as girls of that age often do, Sarah soon had him eating out of her hand. Meanwhile Gavin was suffering, not just from the pain in his injured hand, but also the ache in his heart which only increased every time he saw Sarah fawning over Davie. By bed time that night, his distress was such that he sneaked out of the house and walked up to Jedburgh Road to see if he could find the old woman.

As he turned the bend in the road, he glanced over the hedge and winced in pain as his eyes picked out the two ouch-trees. They were too well-named. Gavin had no idea which house was Araucaria's, but just before the entrance to Victoria Hospital, he heard a meow and, following the sound, he spied a black cat sitting on the threshold of one of the last houses on the road. Plucking up courage, Gavin approached the front door, only to see it open and the old woman standing waiting.

-Come in, Gavin. I've been expecting you.

The young man got to the point immediately.

-OK. I don't know exactly what you are or how you do what you do, but my day with Sarah was the best day ever and I want more. Much more. Can I have longer than one day?

-Of course you can, my dear, Araucaria replied. How long would you like? A week? Two weeks?

-No, I need longer. If you give me a year, it'll be enough time to persuade her to never leave.

-You know what the cost will be, Gavin. Do you think you could pay the price?

Gavin assured her that he would do absolutely anything to make Sarah his. The old woman excused herself for a moment, left the room and came back a few minutes later with another phial of liquid, similar to the one he'd given Sarah a day or two earlier.

-Now this potion is very, very strong, my boy, but it works just the same. Two hairs, one each from you and Sarah, and once you've paid for it, if she drinks it, she'll be yours for a whole year. The rest will be up to you. Meet me tomorrow at eleven down by the ouch-trees and we'll mix the potion.

Gavin promised he'd be there and went back home, optimistic about the future with Sarah but apprehensive about the price he would have to pay. As fate would have it, Sarah was absent from school the next day and Gavin was in a panic until he heard that the usual friends were all to meet in the bowling-green that evening at eight for a party around a campfire. Davie confirmed Sarah would be there. Gavin knew what he had to do.

That evening, the group of friends all climbed into the bowling-green, a fire was lit using paper and twigs, and alcohol and vapes made their inevitable, teenage appearance. But Gavin refused all offers and concentrated on getting close enough to Sarah to get one of her hairs. By the light of the fire, he waited for his moment, sitting behind the girl he loved, and when she put on a set of headphones, he leaned forward and took a hair from the upturned collar of her sports top. Eleven o'clock couldn't come quickly enough for him but thankfully all his schoolmates had long since headed back home, so he was able to push through the hedge and walk up to the ouch-trees unseen.

Araucaria was almost invisible under the wide branches of the nearby sycamore tree. Gavin gave a start when she spoke.

-I thought you might have changed your mind, Gavin. Well done! Do you have the hairs?

Gavin raised his clenched fist to indicate he had them.

-So all we need is the potion to mix them with. There it is, in that pouch, up there at the top of the ouch-tree.

The young man looked up and froze. In the dark, his eyes could barely make anything out but he knew the old woman would be telling the truth.

-Give me the hairs, dear. Right. Up you go. Or you can just go home of course. And remember, no noise. The ouch-trees will get angry.

Gavin braced himself then dived into the branches of the tree, allowing the needle-sharp spikes to slash his body repeatedly as he climbed the short distance to the top. Only his feet were spared, protected by his expensive trainers. The pain in his head, body and limbs was beyond measure but he finally was able to stretch up and grab the pouch before throwing himself backwards away from the hellish spikes. He crashed to the ground and lay there on his back, in agony but triumphant. His ordeal was over. Araucaria clapped her hands in glee.

-Oh, you are such a determined boy, she said. You deserve to have the girl.

Gavin was just about able to hand the pouch with the phial to the old woman. She took out the phial, uncorked it, mixed the hairs with the liquid then crouched down and put it in his blood-soaked hand.

-There, you've paid for the spell and the potion is now active, Gavin. Sarah will soon be yours, she said. Goodbye and good luck! Come on, puss. Let's leave this young man to get on with his life. I'm glad we were able to help. The black cat meowed and Gavin imagined he heard it say "Good luck!".

At that, Araucaria and her cat faded into the darkness, leaving Gavin to return home slowly and painfully to tend to his many wounds in secret.

The next day at school, Gavin had to lie to friends and teachers about his multiple cuts and scratches, saying that he'd tripped and fallen into a gorse bush. The boys all thought it was quite funny but the girls were a lot more sympathetic. Once again, Gavin was able to pour the liquid into Sarah's water-bottle unnoticed during their Physics lesson, but this time she didn't take a drink from it until they were out in the corridor. As she tipped her head back and gulped down a mouthful, Davie came out of the adjacent classroom, saw her drinking and grabbed the bottle from her.

-Perfect timing, Sarah. I'm sooo thirsty, he said before taking a huge swig from her bottle.

-Pig, the girl shouted. You're such a pig! Get your own water-bottle. I suppose you think because you lent me your tracksuit top last night when it got cold, that I'm somehow in your debt. Well I'm not! Sarah punched Davie playfully on the arm but strangely enough he made no effort to defend himself. He was smiling and staring wide-eyed at Gavin.

9

DOGS

Roy was the first to react to the message although everyone got the call at the same time. His first thought was disbelief, but the message left him in absolutely no doubt that his friend Derry was in deep trouble. As he rushed over from the tennis courts towards the road through the park, he was aware of the others starting to react and moving if they could in the same direction. Roy was very disturbed by what he heard and tried to confirm if it was true, but he received no reply and feared the worst.

"He's kicked me in the head. I'm dying".

Roy pulled up about 10 metres short of his friend's body lying on the path under the eucalyptus tree, and turned away to see who else had responded. There were plenty who had heard the horrific message but of course not everyone had been in a position to go over. In fact most of them could only look across the expanse of grass and hope for the best. But deep down, they all knew that Derry wasn't exaggerating. When you say "I'm dying" that means you are. His assailant was still standing over his body, shouting and swearing that he hadn't meant to kill him but merely frighten him away. It was clear from the outset that he saw himself as the victim in this matter and that Derry had brought things upon himself by the manner in which he had approached him. But Roy saw it in completely the opposite way. Didn't he know the difference between a dog attack and a friendly advance? Couldn't he see the eyes, the ears, the mouth and the tail, all of which just said "Do you want to play?"

It was clear that Derry was gone. Nothing could be done for him and the man was already hastily walking away towards the block of flats on Pentland Crescent where he lived with his own German Shepherd. Roy slunk up to the inert body, sniffed it for any sign of life, and even nudged his wee friend with his nose in the vain hope of breathing new life into him. Nothing. And suddenly Roy got angry, How could this happen? Derry was harmless and they all knew he was. How could anyone consider this tiny dog as anything other than an amusing pet, so keen to make people happy. It was unacceptable that a man could kick a dog and leave it dead on a pathway. There ought to be some kind of retribution. There had to be. And the decision was made there and then. Roy was not going to let this go.

He padded away from the growing crowd of people gathering around the body and had his usual sniff at the foot of the waste bin next to the rhododendron bushes. He detected that Lara, Molly, Bruno, Ziggy and Poppy had all been by quite recently and, despite the anxious calls of his owner Bob, still waiting back at the tennis courts, decided he would go and find the others one-at-a-time and see what they thought. Raising his head from path level, he saw that Bruno and Poppy were still within sight, both on the lead and walking quietly around the rose garden with their owners, but frequently glancing back towards the eucalyptus tree where Derry was lying. They responded to Roy's message by going into pipi mode, stopping every few metres for a concerted sniff around followed by a brief leg up or squat. Their owners became a bit tetchy but the stalling tactic gave Roy the time to enter the rose garden, and talk to the two friends personally.

"We've seen the way he treats his own dog Hannibal. He's a bully and a brute, and now he's killed Derry. We can't let him away with such behaviour. He needs to be taught a lesson"

"I agree and I'm willing to help put him in his place" said Bruno the Scotch Terrier. Poppy wasn't quite so keen to get involved in any nonsense that might lead to her friends getting hurt, but the sound of Derry's owner screaming as she ran across the grass to her dear pet's body was enough to change the greyhound's mind. "OK, I'm in." Within ten minutes, Roy had managed to catch up with Molly, Ziggy and Lara, stand nose to tail with each and persuade all three that something had to be done. The wailing and sobbing coming from Mrs. Clark was hugely upsetting for all the other dogs who discreetly let their owners know that it was time to go in.

Roy's priority however was to stay in his master's good books, so he grabbed a stick between his teeth and hammered back over to the area of the tennis courts where Bob was impatiently awaiting his return. The dog greeted his owner with such wonderful enthusiasm and devotion that Bob quickly forgave him for being away for so long and not responding to his calls. Roy knew he would and made continuous eye contact with him until the inevitable treat came out of a pocket and was tossed into the air. The cockapoo jumped high and caught it almost at its zenith then took his place against Bob's right leg for the short walk home. He had a lot of thinking to do that evening.

When it came to thinking things through, Roy was the best dog in the West End. He'd lain down in his bed basket many times before and slowly worked out the best tactics to get what he wanted, be it how to get his favourite treats or how to persuade his owners to let him stay where he wanted. It was mainly eye contact and lolling tongue combined with ridiculous licking and that high-pitched whimpering that almost sounded like a baby crying. Owners were suckers for that. While some dogs might have been lucky enough to do these things instinctively, Roy had had to observe and take note of what others did to get their own way. And that was his strength. He watched, he remembered and he experimented. He didn't forget to come over as your typical stupid mutt, loving his owner way more than he or she deserved and responding instantaneously to that old "sit" "stay" "paw" thing that made most dogs laugh.

By the time Bob was up and ready to take him for his morning constitutional, Roy had the basics worked out. They would give Hannibal's owner such a fright that he would never be bad to a dog ever again. That however meant getting Hannibal onside as well, and he had no guarantee the German Shepherd would betray his owner. He had to find out. So the next time he saw them out walking, Roy worked his way round beside them and ensured that the two owners would get into some sort of "doggy" conversation by letting Hannibal play fight with him.

"We need to talk," Roy messaged. "Your master killed Derry and a lot of us are pretty angry about that. We're going to give him a fright. Are you with us?"

"Sure thing" messaged Hannibal. "I put up a good pretence, but I really hate the bastard. He's a moron. Thinks he's a hard man. Just tell me what the plan is and I'll go along with it."

"OK. I'll get back to you in the next couple of days once I've talked to the others. Now, give an angry bark or two and that'll make them split up."

Hannibal obliged his smaller but cleverer friend, and the two dogs were taken away in opposite directions. Roy spent the next few days working out the plan and sharing it with the other dogs. It was agreed to have a go the following Sunday when all five would make a point of being out at the same time if they all gave the impression they needed taken out.

That Sunday, Hannibal messaged his colleagues at about 11.30 a.m.

"I'm really needing to get out now so I'm about to sneeze and let him know. He'll get the message and take me out. She's at work in Lidl and the boy's away with his pals, so it'll have to be him. He'll take me on his usual circuit of Balgay Park, so I'll keep an eye out for you. Be ready to slip the lead or just bolt when Roy says so"

As Roy wandered by the tennis courts free of the lead, he messaged the team of five to check everyone knew what to do. They all confirmed they knew when to leave their owners and meet up. Roy's plan was a simple one. Get him somewhere on his own, really scare him and hope he learned his lesson. No need to actually harm him. Just make sure he started to show respect instead of treating dogs like shit. It would just be a question of a bark here, a nip there and a warning that dogs can bite back.

Hannibal's role was to get the bully somewhere quiet. So, instead of leaving the path and turning for home at the far end near the bandstand, he kept pulling round to the right where the road climbs steeply towards the observatory. His master swore at him as he always did when the dog was disobedient and gave him a couple of smacks with the lead. But Hannibal put up with that for the umpteenth time and persisted in pulling towards the hill. Once he'd won that battle and they were walking uphill, Hannibal messaged the rest that he'd give a signal as soon as it appeared they were alone on the hill.

With it being Sunday lunchtime, there were plenty other dogs and their owners on the road up the hill. As each passed, they gave Hannibal a knowing nod and a deep growl to let him know they'd listened in and knew what was coming. Twice Hannibal made to send the message to begin the attack but both times a new dog walker came into view and he had to tell the others to stand down again. Roy began to have doubts: maybe it had been a mistake to choose a Sunday. There were too many people walking the dog because they didn't have to go to work. Monday would have been better.

Then it started to rain. As usual, this was a clear signal to all the owners to turn for home and get back before they got soaked. Hannibal sensed an opportunity so, no longer on the lead, he bounded over to the thick bushes at the bottom of the left-hand slope and started rummaging around, as if trying to sniff out a rabbit. Ignoring his master's growing anger and impatience, he kept glancing up to check the road above and below them. And suddenly they were alone.

"Let's do it" he messaged "but be quick." In a flash Roy, Lara and Molly were off over Balgay Park racing for the road up to the Observatory. Poppy slipped her leash cleverly and tore across from the rose garden while Ziggy the black Labrador had to momentarily feign an injury to get his owner to drop the lead, leaving him free to dash off through the cemetery and over to the road. Bruno made an effort to get free but his owner held firmly onto his lead and it was impossible to join his friends. The other five dogs ran up the hill together and slowed as they approached their target. When they reached him they spread out around him in a semi-circle, sat down and waited for a reaction.

The bully knew something wasn't right as soon as he saw five dogs without their masters. He picked up a piece of branch to defend himself, backing off to the edge of the slope. On Roy's command, the dogs began to bark as loudly as they possibly could, but the arrogant man gave a dismissive laugh and started to wield the stick from side to side. Poppy went first, dodging the weapon and grabbing his left ankle, sinking her teeth in hard and escaping before the next swing. Suddenly the man started to take this all the more seriously and called for help.

"Hannibal! Seize them! Come!" Hannibal thought for a second then simply turned away. "You bastard dog" the bully screamed at him. But that gave Roy the chance to spring forward, grab the wrist of the hand holding the branch, and force him to drop it. Ziggy was onto the other arm at once while Molly was quick to bite the other ankle and make him scream even more, as he crashed to the ground, rolling around on the tarmac and flaying his arms and legs to escape. Lara joined in at this point, got her muzzle really close to his face and gave off the most frightening growl ever. Her eyes said "You know I could tear your face apart, don't you?" He closed his eyes, expecting the bite. And that's when Roy decided to call off the attack.

The dogs all let go and returned to sit in their semi-circle, happy with their work. The man scrambled to his feet, swearing with pain and anger, backed off to the edge of the slope and picked up the branch again. "I'm going to kill every fucking one of you" he roared, almost overcome with rage. But as he raised the heavy stick above his head and prepared to charge, Hannibal came bounding across the road and with an outrageously athletic leap, sprang up and hit his master full in the chest. The man wobbled and tried to regain his balance, arms spinning like windmills, but he fell straight backwards head first and disappeared down the slope. Ten metres down, a sycamore tree broke his fall…… and his neck.

The six dogs approached the edge and stared down at the man's broken body without saying a word. Hannibal broke the silence:

"Oops! I only wanted to frighten him."

10

TREE SEAT

Jack sent the text and made his way to the school office, asked for the 6th year attendance register and signed out at 11.30 am. He gave all the secretaries his usual gorgeous smile, told them he'd be back with his kit for P.E. period 5, and, with an unspoken farewell, he turned and walked out onto the Perth Road. Crossing over to the cemetery gates, he then headed townwards, stopping at the

first bus stop, the one just before Grosvenor Road.
When he heard the familiar ping, he took his
iPhone from his blazer pocket and read the
notification from Hannah. She'd followed his
instructions to the letter and was already half-way
back up the path through the wood leading down
to the footbridge over the railway line. That's
where he'd told her to hide at interval and wait for
his text. Good girl, always did what he wanted. He
continued now into Grosvenor Road, walked up as
far as the Tennis Club and waited just inside the
narrow pathway which climbed steeply up towards
Blackness Road. Just a couple of minutes later,
Hannah appeared round the corner and broke into
a jog as she went to meet him, awkwardly trying to
stuff her own blazer into her school backpack as
she ran, and almost tripping herself up in her
efforts.

When she reached Jack's open arms, the bag and
blazer were tossed to the ground as she threw
herself against his fit body and proceeded to snog

his face off, welcoming his roaming hands with not the slightest complaint. She knew what he liked.

But, being just a bit of a control freak, Jack pushed her away.

"I see you've brought a friend, Hannah," Jack said, indicating the black cat that appeared to have followed her up the road.

"Yeah, isn't she lovely? She's just like Casper that my granny Bridgit used to have. She came up to me when I was waiting in the wood and she seems to have taken a liking to me and followed me all the way here. Are you ok, puss?"

"Well it'd better fuck off, lovely or not. We've not got all day".

Jack took a step forward and the cat shrank back, hissing. The boy swung a foot to reinforce his displeasure and the startled beast dived under the hedge and disappeared.

"That wasn't very nice" Hannah said in the cat's defence. "She was only being friendly. I just assumed you were an animal lover."

"Obviously I'm not" he continued. "Is that a problem?"

For Hannah, yes, it was a problem, but she chose to lower her eyes and shake her head silently.

"Right, let's go" Jack said. "I've found a great place in Balgay Park where we are out of sight and can get a bit of privacy. It's only 10 minutes from here".

The fifteen-year-old felt her heart jump again at the thought. Maybe today would be the day. And it would be with Jack, the handsomest boy in the school, captain of the Under-18s at rugby and the boy all her friends wanted to be with. She grinned. It was *her* hand he was holding as they plodded up the steep slope, stopping every few metres to reattach lips and let their tongues do battle. At one point, her legs almost gave way when she emerged from a clinch and she was struggling to contain herself. Jack of course could detect her mounting excitement and knew there would be no need for his practised way with words to get what he had planned to get.

"Taking sweets from a baby" he thought. "Illegal, yeah, but no problem. Not the first cherry I've taken but she is pretty hot."

Once at the top of the slope, the young man marched Hannah across Blackness Road and up the steps leading into Kelso Street which took them down to the entrance to Victoria Hospital, all the while hand-in-hand but no longer grinding their faces together now they were in the public view. Jack knew not to attract too much attention, the kind two pupils still half in school uniform but out of school during lessons could bring. Unwanted attention could ruin his plans or bring reprisals afterwards. At that thought, he quietly let go of Hannah's hand. Now they could be brother and sister. Without changing pace, Hannah stared up at him and asked what she'd done wrong.

"Nothing. Just act like we're off to the dentist" he replied, almost laughing out loud at how stupid that sounded. She'll go along with it, stupid or not.

Hannah bit her tongue and continued along the road in silence, desperate to take his hand again but frightened to upset him and ruin her big moment. The wind kept blowing her long hair over her shoulders and across her face and she paused to gather the blond mop up into a pony tail.

"No, don't do that. Leave your hair down. I like the way it flies around in the breeze."

Hannah let her scrunchie slip back onto her wrist. If Jack wanted to see her hair fly in the wind, then that's what he would see, even if she found it really annoying. There were more important things to do first.

A few steps further on, a golden Labrador raced across their path in pursuit of an object thrown by its owner. Hannah watched with sparkling eyes as the dog picked it up and turned back in one smooth movement, but it then ignored its owner's call to heel and wandered back towards her, dropping an old tennis-ball at her feet. The look on its face said "I like you. Throw the ball and I'll go fetch". Hannah knew what the dog wanted and stooped to oblige but Jack pulled her away by the arm, scolding her for giving something else her attention. He glanced back at the dog which started to bark loudly just as its owner caught up with it.

"Fucking stupid mutt" Jack muttered under his breath.

Hannah could almost hear her late granny tut-tut in disapproval.

Jack then pulled Hannah off to the right and now she saw that they were heading towards a circular garden with a sunken middle and a path around its perimeter.

"It's in here" Jack said. "It used to be a pond. Dad told me once."

He released her arm and felt for her hand which she was delighted to accept. This must be the private place. She pulled multiple strands of hair from her face and mouth to get a clear view. The garden wasn't as private as she had imagined it would be, and indeed it was almost completely open on three sides, but to the left the path bent behind some bushes to re-emerge some twenty metres later on the right. Jack led her down to the bushes on the corner where Hannah paused to examine the tiny bit of pond that still remained from earlier times. She crouched down to peer below the shallow water, scanning for little fish or tadpoles or even a frog. But there was no sign of pond-life.

"Oh, look, a salmon!" Jack said sarcastically, and his impatient tug on her arm told her he couldn't wait any longer. It was time.

At the far corner of the path, Hannah could see a park bench with an enormous tree overhanging it. It looked like it could crash to the ground at any moment. When they stopped at the bench and he told her to sit down, Hannah knew they would be moving no further. This bench was where it would happen. Maybe not quite as romantic as she had been hoping, but with Jack it didn't matter, did it?

She would quite happily have given herself to him in the middle of the Perth Road if she had to.

As Jack took his place on the bench beside her and beckoned her to sit in his lap, the wind suddenly strengthened, causing the branches above their heads to whip to and fro, as if they were screaming at them. The tree seemed to be perturbed by their presence. But the increased sense of danger simply sent Hannah into overdrive and she let Jack slide his hand up her short school skirt and fondle her there. Suddenly she gasped out loud, not in ecstasy at the boy's groping, but in surprise as a small twig torn off a branch hit her on the head and landed on her school bag on the bench. A pang of anxiety jumped into her mind but she tried to focus on being ready to become a woman. Jack was going to take her. This was going to be wonderful.

"Take your knickers off" Jack growled. "I need to have you. Now!"

Completely taken aback by Jack's domineering tone, Hannah made to do as he had ordered but stopped and watched in amazement as he slipped his school trousers and boxers to his knees. She could hardly believe what she was seeing. Jack Davidson, *the* Jack Davidson, was going to do it to her.

"I said get your knickers off. Hurry, for fuck's sake, before someone comes round and catches us. Come on, Hannah. You're not a cock teaser are you?" That usually did the trick. None of the girls wanted to have the reputation of being a tease as that ruined any chance they would have of getting a steady boyfriend.

But Jack's aggression had only served to drive home the message Hannah had been deliberately ignoring all morning. He couldn't possibly be in love with her if he could be so hurtful in what he was saying to her. In a state of utter confusion, she still lay back on the bench in surrender and made to remove her underwear, shutting her eyes to hide the tears welling up inside them. All she could hear now was the wind crashing through the branches above their heads, followed by a whimper. She held her breath in anticipation of what was to come; too scared to tell Jack she didn't want to any longer. This had all been a mistake.

Sensing the point of no return, Hannah gripped the bench beneath her and prepared. She waited. What was he doing? Why was he not on top of her? Her hopes rose that he'd changed his mind and gone, leaving her there half-undressed. The bastard! She opened her eyes. Jack was there alright, only not next to her. He was hanging in the tree above her, wrapped in branches with one that disappeared down his gaping mouth. His eyes were wide open. Another fierce gust of wind ripped through the tree and the outer branches folded in on themselves. He was gone.

Hannah gasped in horror at what she had just witnessed but a sense of calm quickly overtook her. She took a deep breath and began to adjust her clothing, watched inquisitively by a magpie that had hopped over to the bench. As she stood up, a familiar meowing from below drew her attention and the black cat walked out, head held high. Hannah put her blazer back on, picked up her own and Jack's schoolbags, slung them over her shoulder and walked back round to the small pool on the corner. It was packed full of tadpoles and little frogs. She smiled. Granny Bridgit was right. Mother Nature always looks after her own.